HOW TO SUCCEED AT BUSINESS

I lay down for a long nap. When I woke up, I felt awful. One hot mug of caffinex later, I felt like, if not a new person, a reasonable facsimile thereof.

I decided to skip shaving and headed for the garage, where I tried to figure out what I had done to myself the day before. I now

(1) had two ripening bodies in the back of my van;
(2) was responsible for the theft of a small fortune;
(3) owned a total of three illegal weapons; and
(4) possessed over one hundred stolen antigravity rods.

Needless to say, I felt like going back to bed.

ANTI-GRAV UNLIMITED

Duncan Long

AVON BOOKS ◆ NEW YORK

For Maggie, Kristen, and Nicholas,
with much love

ANTIGRAV UNLIMITED is an original publication of Avon Books.
This work has never before appeared in book form. This work is a novel.
Any similarity to actual persons or events is purely coincidental.

AVON BOOKS
A division of
The Hearst Corporation
105 Madison Avenue
New York, New York 10016

Copyright © 1988 by Duncan Long
Front cover illustration by Ron Walotsky
Published by arrangement with the author
Library of Congress Catalog Card Number: 88-91502
ISBN: 0-380-75357-X

First Avon Books Printing: August 1988

AVON TRADEMARK REG. U.S. PAT. OFF. AND IN OTHER COUNTRIES, MARCA
REGISTRADA, HECHO EN U.S.A.

Printed in the U.S.A.

K-R   10   9   8   7   6   5   4   3   2   1

1

I drove up the gravel shoulder to the edge of the highway and held my breath for a moment as the giant vehicle trained its guns on me. I tried to look friendly. I gave a quick wave to go with my big, fake smile. As the road train thundered past, the gun crew waved back as my van rocked in the wash of the twenty-six car chain of gray-and-black vehicles.

I let out a deep sigh of relief that the gun crew hadn't done a Swiss-cheese number on me and my van. I pulled onto Interstate 70 and quickly matched speed with the road train so I could keep up with it. A steady 150 klicks per hour. We hurtled down the ribbon of concrete traveling westward through the barren, treeless grassland that had been baked brown by the summer sun. Only a few abandoned farms and remnants of fencing showed that men had once lived in the area. The only trouble I had on the road was staying out of the way of the wreckage that bounced alongside us from time to time as an old wreck was swept off the road by the train's cattle guard.

The rest of the trip to New Denver was pretty much uneventful except when the road train smashed through a roadblock and shot up some hi-pees. I hoped they knew what they were doing; the government generally frowned on blowing away their employees. But since the road train kept going without having a fighter plane blow it off the pavement, I decided that the hi-pees must have been renegades. You can't trust anyone on the interstate.

Hours later, we left the grassland and crossed most of

the barren Col-Kan Desert. Soon I saw the shadowy, cloudlike Rocky Mountains before the spires of New Denver came into sight. Gradually, black charcoal piles that had long ago been houses started to dot the rock and sand. These gave way to rows and rows of piles of rubble separated by sand laced with burned bricks, bits of charcoal, rock, and scrub brush. I was in one of the suburbs that had surrounded old Denver in its heyday.

It was hard to imagine what the sprawling city must have been like before the water shortage and the limited nuclear war. The destruction of this city and a few others had also spelled the beginning of the end for the superpowers; filling the vacuum were the international corporations, which took over and formed the world government.

I turned off the interstate with a wave to the tailgunner on the road train and headed down the new silver plastic roadway leading to New Denver. Fifteen minutes later I neared the glass and steel buildings that looked like tall glistening jewels springing out of the desert around the space port. In the distance, a rocket thundered toward some faraway part of the earth; a crackling of hot air sounded as the plume of white smoke and fire lifted the white vehicle.

Driving down the valley formed by the high, needlelike skyscrapers on either side of the street, I parked three blocks down from Kraig and Nikki's high-rise complex.

And waited.

I wanted to be sure that someone wasn't onto me before I headed for my friends' place. After the deaths of my lab team, I didn't want to bring trouble onto anyone else.

Hearing a scratching sound at the window, I whirled around, drew my Beretta, aimed, and nearly squeezed off a shot in a blur of motion. I eased up on the trigger, and the hammer lowered to half cock when I saw the face. My breath came rattling out as I realized that I had nearly shot a bag lady. The scraggly woman had more wrinkles than a prune. She didn't seem to see me; she twitched a little, brushed at the dust on the van window, and then turned away. I decided the light must be shining so she couldn't see me, or my embarrassment, through the heavily tinted windows of the van.

I tried to gulp down my heart, which seemed to be beating in my neck, as the rag-covered lady stumbled on down the street. Finally collecting my wits, such as they were, I stepped out of the van and carefully locked it, shivering in the cold shadow of the buildings. I pulled my jacket down to be sure it covered the pistol stuffed back into my waistband. Yes, I was definitely becoming paranoid. But that gun made me feel a lot safer.

I paused a moment and wondered if my friends could really help me or if I was just dragging two more innocent people into hot water, but I just couldn't see how the Kaisers would be endangered as I approached their building. Surely no one could know where I was.

In front of the condo, I stopped a moment and toyed with my shirt collar while looking into the blue-mirrored front of the building. I glanced as covertly as possible all around me. A few cars hummed by quickly and a modif-horse and rider clomped a block away. The only person on foot was the bag lady, who was now rummaging through a pile of garbage at the side of the street. The bot that seemed to be with her liberated a bit of newsfax as they rummaged in the trash, and the sheet blew down the sidewalk toward me and was swept past by another gust of wind.

I tried to look nonchalant and walked to the portcullis of the crystal building and pressed the call button to Kraig's apartment.

The TV camera along with a remote laser gun swiveled toward me, "Phil?" It was Nikki's voice.

"Yeah. Could I—"

"Hurry up. Get off the street." The door flashed open and I stepped into the small cubicle that was suddenly revealed; the door quickly hissed closed behind me.

"Tenth floor?" the elevator asked and I nodded. It whisked me upward at a speed that made my feet swell as my blood tried to stay at ground level. With a sudden stop that sent the blood back up to my head, the elevator doors opened.

"Tenth floor, the apartment is to your right, number ten eighteen," the elevator told me. I looked down the wide hallway. Ceiling, floor, walls, and doors were all made of the same tough blue mirrored plastic. The doors to each apartment were almost invisible, with only small seams and numbers marking their positions up and down the hall. I stepped onto the mirrored conveyer strip down the center of the hall and counted the door numbers as my infinite reflections and I quickly glided by. I stepped off at 1018 and touched the numbers to announce my presence.

I waited. No doubt they were checking to be sure it was me. Without a sound, the door dilated open and I stepped onto the ocean floor.

At least, it looked like the ocean. Fish, plants, a sunken ship was off in the background, barely discernible through the murky blue of the distance. A wicked-looking shark seemed to be eyeing me from a distant cave. The door closed behind me before I could jump out into the hallway.

Nikki stepped from behind a tall bed of pink coral and waved. "Just a minute . . ." She stepped behind the coral and suddenly everything dissolved as she turned off the 3V. I was standing in a stark, white room with thick white carpeting that looked like fur. The room was windowless and completely bare of furnishings.

"Sorry. You got up quicker than I expected," Nikki said with a smile that turned into a quivering frown. She stepped toward me and, with a sob, was in my arms before I knew what was happening, her body shaking.

My first thought was that she was glad to know I was alive.

"Kraig's gone," she said between tears. So much for my theory.

I could see why Nikki was pretty torn up. Kraig was all she had in the way of family. Nikki was a clone. A modified clone.

Kraig's old man had been a bioengineer. By the time Kraig was fourteen, he was working on his doctor's degree in MKC and knew more than most of his professors about bioengineering. While the other kids were making frogs and dinocows, he—we later discovered—was growing his own girlfriend on the side.

Not just any ordinary girl, either. Nikki had started out as a bit of the marrow from Kraig's bones but was altered to the point that she became almost nothing like him. Kraig had, of course, started by altering the XY pattern of his cells to a double X to make her female. But his major accomplishment was in throwing in a lot of special odds and ends to show just what he could do. The end result was a black-haired, Oriental-looking beauty with a well-built, full-in-the-right-places figure. And she was as smart—if not smarter—than Kraig and had super-fast reflexes. If ever there had been a candidate for a new super race, it was Nikki.

Yet she never lorded it over people. Friendly and attractive, she was the girl you always wished would move in next door but never did. She was also always loyal to Kraig.

Perhaps that was because he'd left her in vitro the four years he worked on his degree (how he kept her a secret from the authorities is beyond me—such work was illegal back when we were kids). When he brought her out of "the vat," as he called it, she was a full-grown woman with the mind of a baby. His next step had been to give her a three-year crash course in growing up using machine and human tutors. Kraig was about the only "family" Nikki had ever known.

By the time I'd finished my schooling, Kraig had turned twenty-one and had made his fortune and retired. (And Kraig had money to spare. He was the guy that perfected the Martian goat and the Aqua-retrofit virus that's used to turn ordinary people into Aquanauts. Yeah, Kraig Kaiser. He's *that* Kaiser, if you hadn't guessed. You can imagine the money.)

But Kraig had become as bored as he was rich and had a nearly terminal case of narcissism; last time I'd seen him he'd become about as boring as he was bored. That was one reason I hadn't seen Kraig or Nikki much over the last few years. Though I considered him a friend, his restlessness made me uncomfortable. And he'd developed a cruel streak that was often vented on friends and especially Nikki. I couldn't stand it and had gradually seen less and less of them.

And yet, he had been my best friend. As for Nikki, I'd never gotten as close to her as I might have liked. It is hard to relate to someone who seems perfect even if they don't act the part.

And now Nikki told her story quickly between crying jags. There wasn't much to it. Kraig had cloned himself—again in secret—and two days before had left with the new clone. He'd given Nikki three days to get out of the apartment and never be seen again.

If that weren't bad enough, the clone was male this time. An exact duplicate of Kraig, only younger. And Kraig had made no secret of the fact that the two were lovers. Certainly the ultimate in narcissism. When I heard it all through Nikki's tears, I had to wonder how Kraig had ever been my friend. Now I felt nothing but disgust for him. Kraig could give scum a bad name.

And poor Nikki. I held her tightly and tried to figure out what to do.

Finally, I pulled away to arm's length, looked into her dark, bloodshot eyes, and said, "Can you make enough to get by as ship's navigator?" She worked for the rocket line and I figured she must be getting top credit these days.

That question resulted in another outburst of crying.

I held her and wondered what else was wrong.

"Oh, Phil. They fired me."

I'd heard that the rocket lines were cutting down but had never connected that to Nikki. As a senior navigator, and a whiz when it came to computers and figuring things out, I'd assumed she'd never have to worry.

"Everything's being automated. No more . . . humans. In the cockpit."

(I made a mental note not to fly anymore in rockets. I knew how dependable bots were. Very. But not all the time. It wasn't too hard to imagine that once in a while a rocket flight might take a quick trip to the wrong destination. Ending up in the ocean rather than your correct destination isn't my idea of a fun-filled flight.)

I held Nikki tightly, then let go because I felt guilty. I was beginning to enjoy the feel of her lush body against mine.

She wiped the tears from her eyes and laughed. "Well at least I'm not dead," she said. "What in the world happened to you. I thought . . ." Her chin started to quiver again.

"Don't cry for me. I'm lucky. And alive."

"Yeah. Enough crying. We're all still alive. Sit down." She kicked some hidden spot on the floor. The carpet twisted about and a couch, which was covered with the same material as the carpet, pushed its way up into the room.

"Let me get cleaned up. I've been packing." She retreated back toward the bedroom.

I sat in the quiet of the apartment for a moment.

The door chimed.

"Could you get that?" Nikki hollered out. "Must be Sasee, from next door. She's been helping me pack."

I got up, fumbled at the door's peephole, and accidentally dilated the door open.

It wasn't Sasee. It was the bag woman I'd seen on the street. But not the way she'd been. Now she cradled a needle rifle in her arm. She pointed it at my navel and tightened her finger on its trigger.

2

I stood there trying to get on my feet to run. I also fumbled with the door control but couldn't get the thing to close with her standing in the doorway. Automatic safety device. It made things safe for her, not for me.

Finally, my body got the message and I dived to the side just as her finger twitched on the trigger of the rifle. Though the gun itself made little more than a whishing sound, the tiny needles it fired raised a racket as they broke the sound barrier. They made loud cracking sounds followed by the sound of broken plastic as they crashed into the wall.

She coolly turned and fired a second burst. I was on all fours, dog paddling on the carpet toward the couch as she trained the weapon on me. The needles chewed up the carpeting behind me then clanged against the couch as I got behind it. I had lucked out; the couch was lined with some mechanical device and stopped the tiny projectiles.

I fumbled with the Beretta, which had put a gash in my stomach when I'd hit the floor. Once it was out of my waistband and in my hand, I peeked from behind the couch. The bag lady started a run toward me as another stream of needles bounced off the couch. Now I wished I'd plugged the old bat on the street by mistake.

I heard her hit the couch with one foot and I fired twice as she jumped over it and went hurtling by me.

One of the bullets caught her on the left side of the head as she hurtled through the air. She flopped down on the floor. Apparently her fall released another piece of furniture for, a moment after she dropped, a chair rose up under her and she sprawled over it like a broken rag doll.

"What's going on out here?" Nikki said as she stepped into the room. She was clothed only in a white towel that contrasted with her smooth, dark skin.

"Uh—look out," I cried. The bag lady was moving. A crack showed down her face with a large dimple where my bullet had hit. "She's got armor on. Get back."

Nikki retreated down the hall and around the corner. I pumped four more bullets at the bag lady then decided to camp out behind the couch again. A swarm of hot needles chewed up the wall to my left as I dropped.

A Beretta 92-F pistol holds a lot of ammunition. Fifteen rounds in the magazine; and I kept a sixteenth in the chamber of the ancient pistol. And body armor can't take multiple hits very well from a large handgun. But the chances of hitting the exact same spot twice are small. The three or four times needed are almost impossible to achieve, even at such close range.

But the pistol was the only thing I had so I decided to make the best of it and hope for several lucky shots.

Things were quiet and I figured she was ready to make another charge. Suddenly the room was again filled with the ocean as she turned on the 3V.

Great.

I peeked out from behind the couch and squinted through the water that a small school of rainbow-colored fish was swimming through. The bag lady was nowhere to be seen. I ducked back and rolled toward the outer wall until it stopped my movement. Even though there seemed to be a limitless expanse behind me, I knew there wasn't. Only the 3V projection. I knew that she wasn't behind me.

OK, Now, where is she, I wondered.

A shark darted to my left. I looked back to a large octopus. Her ragged yellow dress stuck out from behind it.

I fired three times through the octopus then rolled behind the large, pink fan coral. Just before I got there, I saw the bag lady fall, hold her head a moment, then straighten up. I might not be stopping her but she'd have a whale of a headache, I thought, and fired another three shots.

I made a dash for where I hoped the couch was. A rain

of needles followed me and licked through the heel of my right shoe. Finding the couch by feel, I dropped behind it, safe for a moment. I peered out and fired two more rounds at the bag lady, who was standing in plain sight on the ocean floor. She stumbled as both bullets hit her. I took careful aim and placed two more hits on her face and saw a bit of her mask break away.

I held my breath and watched as she again fell. Then she struggled to get up again. One tough old battle-ax.

I crouched out of her sight. My Beretta was locked open. Empty. The only box of shells left for it were back in the van. I peeked around the couch. The bag lady was slowly getting up again.

The door? Maybe. Where was it? I looked around and could see only endless ocean with a small saucer sub in the distance. I turned back, and she was standing over me.

I froze. Her broken plastic ballistic mask fell away as she tugged at it to reveal a leathery, wrinkled face with a number of red welts and a cut where my bullets had hit her mask.

Her rifle moved up from my navel to my face. At least it will be quick, I thought. She suddenly got a funny, twitchy grin on her twisted mouth. I waited for a swarm of needles to rip off my face.

Instead, her head rolled off her shoulders. Her decapitated body stood for a moment, spurting blood, then crumpled. It didn't look like she was having any fun at all.

What happened? I wondered.

The ocean faded out and I was again in the living room with a grinning scarred head at my feet. I stepped back as blood soaked into the thick carpeting.

"Sorry I took so long," Nikki said, trying not to look at the body.

She stood in the hallway with a power laser. The beam had been deadly if invisible. "It took a while to find where Kraig had stored this. And I didn't want to cut too low and . . . hit you by mistake."

She put the laser down on the couch and was crying again, back in my arms. And I was ready to add a few sobs of my own.

Ten minutes later, Nikki was cried out and I was at a

loss as to what to do next. Run? Looked like I'd have to; bag ladies don't just go berserk for the fun of it. Not with all that garbage down there on the street.

Nikki? Undoubtedly she was in great danger, too.

I led her into the kitchen. "Look," I said, "I've managed to get you into the middle of things. These—people, whoever they are, knew I was coming, or were waiting for me. . . . They play for keeps. You're going to have to lie low for a while. Or something . . . Hell." I didn't even know what to say.

"What's going on, Phil?"

Good question. I explained what had happened during the last few days.

3

It all started when Hanley Weisenbender stomped into the sunlit lab (when Hanley comes into a room, it's kind of like having a normal person walk out). "What in the world are you doing in here this early?" he'd said.

Normally, he's after me for being late—he thinks I get paid by the hour rather than for thoughts and ideas. Putting me down for being in the lab early was one of the few times he's ever engaged in creative thinking.

"Uh . . . I've been here since last night. We've made a fantastic breakthrough—"

"Forget it. We gave the pink slips to your crew on their way out last night. Here's yours."

"Wait a minute, sir. There's something—"

"Forget it, Hunter." (After working there for six years, we were still on a last-name basis.)

While I stood tongue-tied, Hanley looked past the electronic equipment, magnetic bubble smelters, and bots, directly at the rods. There they were, floating in a group about eight centimeters off the ground, swaying slightly with the air movement in the room. They were anchored by chains, but it was obvious to anyone who cared to study them that they were floating. He looked right at the rods and didn't even blink.

"Stow this junk and get cleared out by noon."

"But—" I sputtered.

"No back talk. That's how it is."

I decided to take a new tack. Hanley's a stickler to the compulsive second power. I tried a proper-paper-work-and-forms angle. "I'll need to get the inventory and records straightened out. . . ."

"The new owners are closing up your section. We're to junk your equipment; sell it for scrap. World tax write-off. Get your personal stuff and be out by noon."

So much for my paper-pusher strategy.

I was in shock. Here was the greatest breakthrough since fire (in my humble opinion) and Hanley the cave man was going to pass it up.

I was also a little mad.

While I stood doing a quiet meltdown, he checked the dust on the clear silicon counter like he usually does—my crew says that's a carryover from his military space service—and turned to leave the lab. "Pick up the rest of your month's pay on your way out," he said over his shoulder. The labbots didn't get pay chips so I figured he must have been talking to me.

"Now what?" That was what I thought and I guess I even said it to the empty room when Hanley left.

Who would have thought that while I'd worked through the night a takeover deal had been arranged by World Energy halfway around the world? Blasted corporations had taken over the world and now they were shuffling it to play their games. While I perfected and put the final touches on the rods, a group of men in expensive glow suits had probably been signing away each member of my group.

I guess it isn't too surprising.

Our whole end of things had been developed as a pet project of the chairman of the board, who retired a year after initiating the project because she went senile. That no doubt looks bad on paper.

And if I hadn't been in the middle of our project, I would have thought our antigravity lab was probably next door to the UFO research bureau and the grow-hair-on-cue-balls research lab.

OK.

But the hell of it is that the "Yes sir, no sir, cover my posterior" guys probably missed the greatest chance for money since the Arabs sold their oil fields at the points of Russian bayonets.

After Hanley Weisenbender had broken the news to me, I was tempted to call some of the higher-ups and tell them what kind of a mistake they'd made. But then I got to thinking about how things always work out.

No matter who I work for, I always lose my job. And this time my crew of lab assistants—who'd become good friends—had lost theirs as well. All because some group of money grubbers didn't have the sense to check out what they had and some manager like Hanley Weisenbender couldn't look past the dust on the tables to see what was floating under his fat nose.

Somewhere during those few minutes, I decided to go into business for myself. Antigrav, Unlimited.

Hanley had managed to give me some interesting information and I had the other chunks to put into place: (1) No real inventory would be taken of the lab, (2) my crew didn't know if we'd succeeded or not, and (3) I was really the only one who knew that the rods existed and worked.

My plan was simple but a little hard to pull off: Steal everything I could.

First I supervised the bot while he got the last load of rods out of the molds (without launching any more!) and got them clamped to the other rods floating in the room.

Maybe I should explain a little so you'll know what makes the rods so wild to handle. (No, no boring science lecture, just the basics.)

The antigravity rods are a lot like bar magnets. Only instead of having a north and south pole, they have positive and negative gravity at each end. One end is attracted to normal matter while the other end is repelled by matter. Yeah, sounds crazy but that's how it works. (If you want to come by and spend a week with your compucalc, I'll show you the fundamental concept—but remember we'd been working full-time for six years to get these things straightened out.)

My lab team had thought things out before I ever started making the rods the night before I was fired. The rods were quite dangerous. They each weighed about fifty kilograms if the plus side were pointed toward the earth while they could lift about fifty kilograms if they were pointed up (more if there was something over them). But you have to remember that for every action there's an opposite reaction; we're not dealing with magic here.

That means that if you happened to get your foot under one of the rods that was trying to lift off just a few inches from the ground, your foot would be pinned under it by the fifty kilogram push. Have a bunch of them hover near your head and you could be crushed!

They weren't for fooling around with.

Likewise, if two—one up, the other down—were put on a pole that pivoted in the center, you could have a virtual perpetual motion machine. The catch was that it was pretty hard to get them stopped. And if the pivot burned out (as it quickly would since all that kept the rods' speed down was the friction of the air), well it wasn't safe to be in the area when the things took off at who-knows-what speed. And if you stood close by while your perpetual motion machine was running, the force waves could literally beat you to death.

Now you know what I had—something as dangerous as a swimming pool of nitroglycerine but also capable of making almost endless free energy if correctly harnessed.

Even though I was aware of how dangerous the things were, I was fuming from Hanley's visit and was getting tired, punchy, and careless—so when the last group of rods were released from the mold, one rod departed right through the roof leaving a hole the width of the rod. (I spent a few tense minutes waiting for a plane or pleasure dirigible to come crashing down. Fortunately for all involved, none was overhead.)

After a quick check of the vidtables, I found that the moon and all listed manned stations were not in its path (as near as I could figure—I was never too patient with plotting those things). Provided the rod made it past all the spy eyes, it was beyond worrying about—I hoped. I tried to be a bit more careful after that.

I'd been fastening the rods together. One rod up and one down so that they had a weight only equal to the fasteners. The last rod was then fastened to counteract the weight of most of the connectors so the whole thing weighed about five kilograms (though it still had the real physical sideward mass of the rods).

So I then had the rods. All I needed now was my van. And a friend who—I hoped—was on duty as the head security guard. I made a quick call on the vidphone.

Ralph answered. I was glad to see him but tried to hide it.

"Hi, Phil," he said. "Sorry about the job."

"That's part of the game," I said, trying to look the part of the forlorn rather than the criminal element. I haven't done anything crooked—except maybe for last year's regional tax form—since cheating on my second grade computing quiz. But Ralph didn't seem to notice anything wrong. Or maybe he was hoping I'd even things up.

"I'll be needing to bring my van around to the side door to get some stuff packed, Ralph. Any problem?"

"Nope. I'll pass the word. And"—I held my breath; please no inspection on the way out—"keep in touch, Phil."

"Yeah. Will do."

"And good luck."

"Thanks." I knew I'd be needing it.

A few minutes later I had my blue van parked at the side door. I managed to get it there without running over anyone or wrecking it. To say I was a little nervous would be an understatement. Between the two days without sleep, liters of caffinex, and my lack of practice at being a criminal, I was a little shaky.

Once back in the lab, I felt like a kid at Christmas. It's one thing to work with expensive equipment day after day, quite another to take it home with you. The main thing was to pick what I needed and what wouldn't be missed. I figured that if Hanley Weisenbender thought I'd taken anything, he'd personally lead the commando raid on my house. I had to split the difference between being overly cautious and bloodsucker greedy.

We had about eight computers and umpteen compucalcs; in went three compucalcs and two computers (which I told to shut down so they wouldn't chatter to me when I drove through the checkpoint later on).

What next?

I plugged a power cable into my van's batteries. Might as well use a little power for my last day at work.

Then a lot of odds and ends of equipment that I thought I might need, one labbot (a very small one—the space in the van would be a bit tight with the rods), a whole box of notes that hadn't yet been given to the computers to read, and a nice array of tools—including the laser cutting/welding torch—went into the van.

The tricky part was getting the rods into the van. They weighed five kilograms if they didn't get tilted. There was a little leeway, but if they passed the point of no return, they went from weighing five kilograms to almost a thousand! I didn't want to let them tip over in the van. The disaster would be hard to explain if I survived the experience.

So two of the large labbots and I inched them into the van after I had checked to be sure no one was around to see what was going on. The bots helped me anchor the rods in the van. Then I shut down all the bots in the lab.

By 11:30 I was finished. I looked around. "OK, what did I forget?"

My pay chip for the rest of the month. I needed that. It was crazy, but while I had a bit of priceless technology in my van, there was no capital to work with. Especially since my Mastivisa account was in borrowed-to-the-quick condition. And I knew my local friendly electric banker wouldn't be giving me a loan to work on a whacko idea like antigravity devices.

A few moments later, with pay chip in my hot fist, I headed around the huge plastic bubble that formed the lab and administration complex, got into the van, and—very carefully so that the rods wouldn't break loose from their moorings—eased toward the front gate, which was the only exit through the mass of mines and electrified barbed ribbon surrounding me.

That's where things started looking bad.

Ralph wasn't there; in his place swaggered Frank Small, whom my staff maintained was Hanley Weisenbender's bastard son. They were half right at least. And if anyone would make an effort to go through my van and give me fits, it was Frank.

I slowed down very carefully.

"Hear you got canned," he smiled.

"Yeah."

"I'm surprised they didn't do it sooner."

I smiled a weak grin. I'm pretty good at boot licking when it might keep me out of jail.

"I need your badge and compukeys."

At this point I was hoping Frank couldn't smell fear. I tried to swallow and couldn't. "I turned them in. At the front desk when I picked up my pay chip," I gulped. Here he was worrying about next to nothing while I was trying to sneak out with the crown jewels. I looked at my scared face reflected in his mirrored glasses.

I don't know why, but instead of playing it cozy, I added, "Go ahead and check, you'll just be wasting your time."

That riled him a little. "Yeah, we'll see." He turned to the vidphone and told it what extension to contact for the head desk. He murmured to it for a few moments while I wished I had a machine gun to try out on his fat rump.

He turned back with a look of sheer disappointment. "OK. What's in the van?"

My last smart answer had paid off, why not try again?

With a big fake smile, I told the truth, "A stolen labbot, two computers, several boxes of lab tools, and antigravitation rods worth more than anyone can probably imagine. Want to look?"

He didn't even glance toward the back of the van. Lucky for me he couldn't see into its dark interior with his sunglasses. He gave me his worst snarl and waved me through.

We probably both thought good-bye and good riddance. But I had the valuables and he only had the bad taste in his mouth.

The noon Kansas City traffic leading to my home was the usual hassle. All the crazies were out with the usual unipeds, bikes, modif-horses—and one blue van. All the while I was trying to accelerate/brake without causing the massive rods to come loose and either drop out the back doors of the van or come sliding forward and crush me. If I had to choose between driving those things through rush-hour traffic or juggling primed RAW grenades, I'd go for the grenades every time.

I was doing well until I almost smacked into the robed figure of a Dweller on a bicycle when he suddenly cut into the van's path. As I bore down on him, it was the first time I've ever seen one of those guys show any emotion; also the first time I've ripped anyone's robes off his back when passing!

No police unipeds or traffic eyes were about so I just speeded up a little and left the guy before he could collect his wits and get my van's tag number.

I was very, very glad to get to my little green bubble dome and open the garage door with my scramble coder. If I'd been more alert I would have noticed the bars had been pried off the side window with the finesse of a cosmetic surgeon using a machete. But I was too preoccupied for the sight to register.

When the plastic garage door closed behind the van, I opened my van door and heard the intruder alarm inside the house. Great. I quickly closed the van door.

The house system gives off a false alarm about once a month (which is why I removed it from the vidphone cable; if the police come, they charge per trip for false alarms, plus you're apt to get on their blacklist). I was cautious but had that old "it can't happen to me" attitude. Nevertheless, I reached down under the driver's seat of the van and pulled out the plastic bag that contained my old Beretta 92-F nine-millimeter automatic pistol.

Now before you go moral on me, I know that having a firearm is illegal. But if you're fair, you'll also admit that just about everyone has an unregistered one squirreled away somewhere. I'm no different from the next guy.

So I pulled out the weapon and clicked off the safety (I always carry it with a round in the chamber, ready to fire once the safety is released).

While I was fumbling around with the pistol, the door from the dome to the garage opened and two "gentlemen," who were unmistakably pukers, stepped through. Mohawks, flowered shirts, chains . . . you know the look. They acted like they owned the place. Maybe they did.

And there I sat in the van, trying to look invisible.

Since the alarm was blaring in the house, they had apparently not heard me come into the garage. Lucky for me since they were armed; one had an old Colt AR-15 assault rifle—old but deadly—and the other had a three-shot rail gun. In my book, an assault rifle and a rail gun beat out one pistol. Especially a pistol manned by someone who hadn't ever fired the thing in anger.

Pukers aren't noted for leaving behind breathing victims. And these guys didn't look like they'd be leaving without checking out the van. I couldn't race out of the garage without the rods crunching around—which would be even worse then anything the pukers could do—so I was going to have to take care of the guys or get shot trying.

I sat tight, slumped down in the van, sweat pouring out of my armpits. I slowly opened up the side vent on the van, waited, and prayed my "please God, just this once" prayer asking that they would walk over where I could get a clear shot at them.

They took their time and didn't cooperate at all with my brilliant tactic.

After an eternity, they headed toward the front of the van, walked past (whew . . . without looking in), and started pawing through the tools on my work bench.

That also lined them up with my open window vent. Ever so quietly and carefully, I brought my Beretta up to the window and tried to aim at the one carrying the rail gun. Aiming is not easy when your hand is doing a little jig out on the end of your arm.

I jerked the trigger and down went one while I screamed from the painful noise—magnified inside the van—of the pistol.

Fortunately, the puker wasn't too bright. Or maybe he just hadn't watched the right 3V ads. At any rate, the one left turned and brought up his rifle and proceeded to spray the van's windshield with automatic fire.

Like most other folks who could afford it, I had gotten a van with carbopolythene glass. It's just as tough as the ads say, and—as proved by my independent, highly personal, puker tests—bullet proof. If the puker had fired through the door or side windows, I would have had it. But he only fired at the windshield.

After a few noisy moments, he was standing there with an empty rifle. He stood with his mouth hanging open and I sat in the van with my jaw clenched shut. Suddenly he went for his partner's weapon and I fumbled with the vent window, finally got it open, and fired three times. He crumpled.

After the spectacle was over, I carefully got out of the van and enjoyed the dry heaves while my ears rang.

Most people would tell you I'd made the world a better place since two pukers were dead. But I would not be truthful if I didn't tell you that I was more than a little upset; this was the first time I'd actually had to defend myself and I didn't relish it.

Legally you can kill anyone who's in your house unin-vited. At least you can in our region. Also, using an unregistered weapon to do it is not too big of a deal so far as the police are concerned when the end result is two dead pukers.

But I also had a load of stolen rods and equipment. And I really couldn't afford to take the next few days filling out forms, telling compupolice my life story, and maybe even feeling the wrath of other pukers should they find out what I'd done.

So I calmly got two body bags out of the locker in the garage and filled them up.

Maybe you're wondering why I happened to have two body bags.

I traded for them on the black market after I'd talked to a friend who had reported a killing to the police. I didn't care to go through the ordeal myself after hearing of the hassle. Life is just too short and the government already does its part to make it as tense as possible.

At the same time, don't think I was callous about this. I still had a bad case of the shakes and these were the first dead bodies I'd ever had the pleasure of working with and hopefully the last, thank you.

I finally got the guys zipped up and—with a lot of straining on my part—pulled the two bags into the corner of the garage for the time being.

That done, I turned off the alarm.

I opened the van and could have kicked myself for straining with the bags—the labbot was sitting right there waiting to move at my beck and call. Some days I could give absentminded scientists a bad name.

"Labbot 3 on," I told the bot. It perked right up and swiveled its camera to look at me. With the tedious instructions needed to control a bot, I got it to do what I wanted, and we managed to move the rods out of the van and fasten them to the side of the garage. Provided we didn't have an earthquake, I figured they'd be pretty safe there for a while.

We—I seem to think of labbots as living entities so I say "we"—unloaded the equipment, and the labbot stuffed the two corpses into the van. I closed and locked it and then had the bot stand in the corner where I covered it with a drop cloth.

I went inside for a long nap.

4

My head felt three times its normal fat size. Guess I must have slept on my face or something. Anyway, when I woke up, I felt awful. It was still gloomy out so I checked my thumbnail watch through blurry eyes; it was *very* early in the morning. But I couldn't get back to sleep—too much to do. And the smell was awful. My clothes seemed to have taken on a life of their own—an existence that could have fit right into an organic barnyard somewhere. So my first order of business was a hot shower followed by two aspers and some clean clothes.

One hot mug of caffinex later, I felt like, if not a new person, a reasonable facsimile thereof.

I decided to skip shaving and headed for the garage.

As I stepped into the garage, I tried to figure out what I had done to myself the day before. I now

(1) had two ripening bodies in the back of my van,
(2) was responsible for the theft of a small fortune in equipment,
(3) now owned a total of three illegal weapons (including the two pukers'), and
(4) was the owner of the 103 stolen antigravity rods.

I felt like going back to bed.

But it was early morning. That was something I needed to take advantage of since that's when the roads are least traveled.

Shortly I was moving down the street in front of my

dome. Driving carefully so that I wouldn't get stopped by a spot check (no drugs, officers, just two bodies), I headed out of the city with its traffic eyes and got onto the interstate.

Two hours later, the body bags were dumped at an abandoned rest stop. I hightailed it back to my house.

Whew.

After getting that over with, I felt like a free man. It is amazing how much pressure was removed when I kicked those two thugs out of the back of my van and returned home without getting stopped.

The alarm was silent when I got back: a welcome change.

After another cup of caffinex and a good-size meal from the instawarm, it was, finally, time to get down to some worthwhile work.

The first project would be creating my own power company. The work I had in mind later was going to take a lot of electrical power and I was already paying an arm, leg, and some other major body parts just to keep the light, 3V, instawarm, and van recharger going. An electrical generator made a lot of sense.

As I soon found out, it would have been easier not to have the labbot jerk the electric engine out of the van; the motor proved a little hard to get back in. Also, I should have experimented with an old motor—if I'd failed at my task, I would have ruined a perfectly good van. But by now, caution had been thrown to the wind. I wanted to get to the nitty-gritty of the practical use of the rods.

After the bot had placed the van's engine on the concrete floor, we went to the corner where the rods were, anchored them more securely in place, removed one, and clamped it on its side to the vise on the work bench.

The idea was to slice off several sections of rod so that they could be mounted on the electric motor of the van. This would enable me to power the van, and since the motor would also become an electrical generator if it moved on its own it would become a source of electricity. (I told you these rods had a lot of potential.)

You'll notice I didn't say "just" slice off several sections of the rod. That's because the force exerted down the length of a rod is pretty great. Though the metal that the rods were made from was relatively soft, if a regular synthadiamond saw were used to cut into them it would soon become all but locked in the gravity field. Though it could be moved, the friction would melt either the rod or the saw blade before the job was done (unless you wanted to take sixteen years doing it or had a waterfall to cool the metal). So I used an industrial laser that I'd "borrowed," compliments of Weisenbender and company.

Even the laser was tricky to use since the rod tended to reflect the light and burn holes in the workbench and me, but the laser did its job fairly quickly.

The bot and I got most of the rod sectioned, though one small piece did get away. It was spinning with a slight wobble when it escaped so that it went twisting off on a zigzag tangent that finally ended when the projectile lodged in the rafters of the garage.

Even the bot followed the action with its unblinking camera eye.

By noon my able—if dim-witted—electronic assistant and I had gotten the lengths of rod welded to the armature of the van's motor. Standing back from the plane they'd be operating in, I crossed my fingers and had the bot remove the restraining chains (I figured I'd rather lose one bot than some important part of my anatomy).

The rods started right up in their tight little orbit and very quickly the shaft was spinning at its maximum speed.

I sprayed it liberally with sililube and started taking measurements of how much electricity and mechanical power the thing was giving off. It put out quite a bit of power. Only then did the full impact of the last six years' work set in. Generators like the one I'd created could be the solution to any number of mankind's energy and travel problems.

Now the cynical among us would probably figure I had wired myself into a corner: the motor was going lickity split without a load on it and the van's motor pod was empty. But it wasn't quite like that. The problem of stopping the motor had—more or less—been planned on.

Remember that the greater the load that is placed on a generator's circuit, the more slowly it tends to turn. Short the thing out and it practically stops. That was the theory. And I had also already connected a load to the motor's shaft just to be on the safe side.

My problem was that the rod-driven generator I'd created from the van's electric motor put out a lot more energy than I'd expected. Shorting the thing out looked a little dangerous and might tend to melt the heaviest of cables.

Finally I got the bot ready to latch onto the motor when I gave the order, then I used a pry bar to short out all the cables I'd connected into the generator.

Somehow we managed to do it without burning down the garage or ripping the bot apart. (Since the gearbox of the van would slow down the motor/generator in the future once the motor was back in the van, getting it stopped if it ever needed to be worked on in the future would be easier once the motor was in place.)

After a short break to collect my wits and replace one of the bot's arms with the spare in its chest, we carefully chained the lengths of rod so they couldn't start spinning, and the motor was placed back in the van. Easier said than done. At this point I realized that I would have saved a lot of time if I'd left the motor in the van and modified it there, but there was no way to undo what I'd done. Many curses and skinned knuckles later, it was back in place.

The motor mounted, the shaft was connected into the transmission and I was ready to say good-bye to the household vehicle transformer (I hoped).

I left the rods locked in place while I removed the batteries from the van. I left one small bank for back-up power, though, in case the rod-driven generator went down. The batteries would do little other than power emergency lights or the like since the motor would probably be shot in such an event and beyond the help of battery power. But I knew the batteries would be useful for the project I had planned several days later.

I cannibalized the van battery charger to create some outlets inside the van for regular household appliances or my shop tools. Finally, I placed a waterproof outlet inside the front bumper so that I could power appliances with electricity generated from the van's motor. With a long extension cord, the van's generator could be used to run household appliances when the van was in the garage—and thereby lower my utility bills (I didn't want to quit using the government's power since that would attract too much attention).

The bot risked life and limb once more to remove the restraining chains and the motor hummed to life. Though it sounded a bit more beefy than a normal van's electric motor, it wasn't strange enough to attract attention—I hoped. (It would be a little strange if I had to park since the motor would continue to hum along when I left it. That would attract notice, so I decided I'd have to figure something out on that count.)

I tested the outlets and found that they furnished all the electrical power I could ever need. The job finished, I stood back and was thankful I didn't own any stock in the major conglomerates. Or—worse yet—was with the group that had decided to sack my team's six years of work. They would be lucky to keep their heads lined up with the proper bodies.

For some reason, that made me realize that I'd forgotten to get in touch with my lab team. They had to be on pins and needles. I had planned on bringing them back together with me but at this point I wanted to keep them in the dark. It would be better for them and my "company" if they thought we'd failed. It might also be a problem to all of us if any of them started trying to stir things up about the antigravity project.

My plan was a little hazy at that point. Basically, what I hoped to do was get a few working examples of the antigravity rods' possibilities cobbled up and then get my team back together. In the meantime, I didn't have the space or money to get the group going. And there was security. I knew that a lot of people would want to get rid of us if they ever found out what we were up to. We stood to make money, but a lot of someones were going to lose a lot. A whole lot. And that doesn't make for friendly feelings.

I figured my best bet was to persuade the members that the project had finally failed but that they should keep in touch so we could restart our project when I finally got some money for continuing.

So before giving the van a test drive, I called all eight of my lab team members during the next hour (Linda was the hardest to get and I spent forty-five minutes tracking her through the telenet). I broke the ''news'' to them that the rods were a dismal failure but that we must be on the right track, we'd get back together soon, keep in touch, etc.

That done I raced back into the garage after a side stop to keep from having kidney failure.

The test of the rod-driven motor in the van was about to begin! I got the bot into the corner, ordered him off, then jumped into the van like a kid on World Freedom Day. Almost backing through the garage door, I remembered to use the scramble coder to open it and—barely containing myself—put the van into reverse and eased out.

It worked like a charm.

I tooled up to the interstate (consciously going the opposite direction from the rest stop that I'd dumped the two body bags in) and tried out the motor's full power for a mile or so. (Luckily no hi-pees were about.)

I quit when the van hit 200 klicks. That's just a little fast, considering that the top speed for a brand-new van is only 80. Besides becoming a bit worried about the thing shaking itself apart on the bumps in the road, it was apt to draw someone's attention. And I figured bureaucratic some-ones would probably like to get their hands on the van to create a new tax category, if nothing else.

So I drove back to the garage at a sedate speed.

With one side trip to a telebank where I deposited my pay chip and then hit my favorite Radio Dome electronics store where I spent every centime I'd deposited. The next step for the van would help me realize one of my longest held dreams. To fly on my own.

Only this time if things worked out the sky would not be the limit.

5

I won't bore you with the details. My team always said I talked them to death. After a while I started to take the hint.

Here's basically what I—and my able labbot—did: We got several of the complete rods and welded them to the frame of the van so that it had an apparent weight of only a few kilograms. That done, we cut about half the rods to manageable lengths (I used the outlets in the van to power the laser), welded the short lengths to the thousand and some military surplus step motors I'd purchased (the clerk must have thought I was trying to corner the market, though he didn't say anything), anchored the motors all over the inside of the van, tried to locate the center of the van for placing the gyroscope, and wired the motors and the gyroscope so that they were controlled by one of the lab computers, which was also securely anchored in the van between the driver and passenger compartments. (Figuring how to place them was harder than wiring them up; they had to go where the combined forces of the antigrav rods wouldn't tear the van apart—that could be embarrassing.)

Even with the labbot doing most of the work nonstop on autoprogram, the work took two days. The next day was spent trying to tell the computer how to control the array of step motors properly. It's one thing to make a van float, it's another to make it float where you want it to. And I also had to make the computer realize that pointing the rods the wrong way could crush the passenger and/or the

computer itself; even the new computers don't have much
sense when it comes to fear.

Suddenly the computer and I both got the hang of it
and there the van was, floating about two feet off
the garage floor. It sort of hovered while several of the
step motors moved back and forth to counterbalance
the whole thing.

It took a moment to sink in: *It worked!*

Before dashing out, I was a little cautious and placed the
other computer in the van. It would be my backup to
control the step motors if computer one failed. (Number
one assured me it wouldn't, but who ever trusted a computer? So number two went in and number one whispered
all its secrets into its little electronic ear.)

I loaded up more tools than I could ever possibly need
in case I would have to make some repairs "on the road"
and hopped into the van. This time I fastened my seat belt
very tightly.

I stayed close to the ground until I got the hang of it.
Though the computers normally work with spoken com-
mands, I was afraid that wouldn't be fast enough so I
had connected the regular controls into the system: The
steering wheel controlled directions, the brakes and
accelerator pedal regulated the speed, the turn signal
became the upward/downward control. The brake lights
and turn signals all went off line when the flying mode
was engaged.

Later that night, a blue UFO moved across the sky and
barely set down to become a van again before three World
Military fighters came screaming through the area looking
for the UFO. They darted to and fro like angry dragonflies
on their flex wings; they hovered a moment, searching in
vain for their prey, then wheeled on a silent command and
streaked out of sight.

I decided to drive home—or at least hover close to the
road. Fighter planes can get mean.

While I was out flitting around, someone blew up my
house.

When I got back, only a pile of burned plastic and black
ash marked the square of land where my dome had been.
The rods I'd left behind in my dome were not to be seen.

They'd undoubtedly headed off into space in fifty different tangents after being freed by the explosion. Bits of the dome and my belongings had dented the domes around it; there was nothing left to claim. If I had been crazy enough to try to claim anything. Someone had played demolition ball with my home. That was when I realized that the project hadn't been canceled by mistake. The whole purpose had been to get us out of sight—then out of existence. I glanced at the rubble that had been my dome, and then got out of the area as fast as I could.

Talk about mixed emotions—one minute I was gliding through the air with the world on a string and the next I felt as if I were a hunted animal.

I stopped at the first Mastivisa vidphone booth and tried to call some of the team members; I figured they were in danger. The machine told me my card had been canceled. I got away from the booth as quickly as I could since I didn't want to be caught by anyone they might send to check me out. At least I was paranoid enough to think they'd send someone. Since I never carried money, I was now homeless and centimeless.

I did have some tools, however, and soon an old-fashioned coin phone had given up its change. Again racing away, I stopped at a third phone to try calling my team members again. None of the members could be reached. All out? It was getting late and I was really worried. What was going on?

I parked the van in a hedge on a back road and slept fitfully with my Beretta across my lap. The next morning the last of my stolen money was spent for a news sheet. The day's plastic sheet carried my death notice along with those of my lab team. No details. I was alive. Were they? I hoped so but knew that it was just by the slimmest of chances that I hadn't been at home in bed when my house had been ripped apart. I had a queasy feeling they had all been killed.

I had other worries, too. There aren't that many vans on the road these days. I knew I stuck out like the milk glands on a dinocow. The first order of business was a trip to Nervous Eddy's. Ed was where I did all my black market business. I hid the van behind his store and walked into the

old concrete building. I stood just inside for a moment so
my eyes could adjust to the dark interior.

Nervous Ed sat on a tall stool behind the front counter.
He looked just as nervous as his name suggested. I always
wondered why he persisted in carrying on his illegal
business—camouflaged as a tool store—if it made him so
jumpy.

"The walking dead," he said with a twitch.

"Yeah, I need some help."

At this point his black sentinel bared its three rows of
teeth and gave a growl that danced up and down my spine.
Ed didn't say a thing to the sentinel but gave a quick hand
signal that made it leap over the counter and stay out of
sight. "What'd ya need and what'd ya got?" Ed chanted,
a tic pulling his leathery face into a scowl.

I was glad I'd left the dome with a lot of extra tools. I
slid two electric wrenches and a compucalc—which I hoped
I wouldn't need—across the scratched glass countertop
toward him. Ed normally doesn't betray any emotion but
he raised one eyebrow at the wrenches. He's a sucker for
electric wrenches.

"I need some tag decals and instapaint. Red and white.
And some swirl controls for the paint."

"You can get most that stuff at a retail store. The
decals are illegal; that's harder," he squinted at me trying
to figure out what my angle was.

"If you have a card; mine's been revoked," I told him.

"You are in trouble."

He thought a moment, then started collecting cans of
instapaint, swirlers, and the illegal tag decals from various
cubbyholes in the store. I've never known Ed to be generous or trade without dickering. The fact that he was pulling out everything I needed without a fuss drove home the
fact that I was in pretty deep trouble and that he probably
wanted to get me out of his store as quickly as possible.

"Anything else?"

I thought a moment and then remembered the magazine
I'd taken out of the puker's assault rifle (which was in
the back of my van). I pulled the magazine out of my hip
pocket. "Got any ammunition for one of these? I need
some more nine millimeter, too."

Ed held the magazine a moment as he studied it, hiked up his old thick spectacles on his broad nose, then handed the magazine back. "Hummm." He turned and sank from sight behind the counter. I heard him rummaging about in a drawer.

"These are hard to come by. Cost ya extra." He shoved three dog-eared boxes of ammunition across the counter toward me.

I fished for a moment in my front pocket for my last barter chip: an electric screwdriver.

Ed's eyes twinkled, "Done . . . and . . ." He reached under the counter. "Here, you'll be needing this, too."

My eyes must have displayed my surprise: a Mastivisa card.

"It's stolen. But should be good for another day or two. Just don't go over fifty at a time. I figure you'll need it."

I didn't know what to say but just nodded. I scooped everything up and headed toward the door. "Thanks, Ed."

"Be careful."

After inspecting the lot behind the store, I backed into the abandoned building next to Ed's. Out of sight, I quickly placed the decals on the tag impressed in my rear bumper. Soon the numbers of a different van appeared on the bumper. It wouldn't pass a check, but if they were looking for my specific tag number, it might get me by. The tag number changed, I set up the instapaint on the swirl pattern controller and painted the latest of bopper designs on the van.

I hoped the van would now look different enough to get me out of the area. I stowed the extra cans and the controller in the van and pulled out. There was just one place to go. I started the long trip with the sound of my growling stomach filling the van.

8

About a full minute into the journey to New Denver, I realized that using the stolen Mastivisa card would get me killed. Using the card would leave an electronic trail that would lead directly to me.

After retracing my route for about fifteen minutes, I crossed back into Missorark under the east side of the old and—in the smog—nearly invisible Kansas City dome. As I traveled under the edge of the giant dome, the blue-green of the city's sky lamps startled my eyes. I darkened the tint of the van's windshield.

Knowing I'd need food, I watched the old concrete storefronts that were interspersed with new plastic buildings and slowed at the first auto-grocery store I came to. Turning, I pulled into the line of vehicles in front of the huge yellow bubble store. Happy Dog Groceries and Supplies.

After waiting in line a few minutes, I eased the van up to the window and pushed the control to open the van window so that I could place my order. My nose was assaulted by the stale fumes of garbage and burned coal that always seemed to float in the decrepit city's air.

"Good evening. Generic or name brands?" the purple dog asked, with a crazy, toothy grin.

I wondered why adults would want to talk to a robot dressed as a dog. "Whichever is cheaper for each item," I answered. I figured paupers with stolen cards had to get the most they could for their money.

"Your list?" the dog asked with a wink.

I gave the bot a quick list of the freeze-dried and irradiated foods off the top of my head since I hadn't thought to make a list while sitting in line. "And a few of my favorite un-sugar candies," I finished.

"Is that all?"

I nodded.

"Total is sixty-five creds. Card?"

Great, I thought. A card can't go over 50 creds without a quick scan. That would be a disaster with a stolen card.

"Uh, I don't have that much in my account," I said with a blush creeping up my neck. "How 'bout cutting it down?"

I could hear the group of vinyl-and-leather-clad bikers just behind my van loudly voicing obscenities. I glanced at them in the rearview mirror to see what kind of brain-dead beings I had to contend with.

"Any preference as to what we remove?" the bot seemed to have lost its mechanical smile.

"No. Anything. Just get the total to . . . uh . . . 48 creds. Leave the candy."

"OK. Card?"

"Yeah," I handed it over. The bot held it in front of its eyes and videofaxed it.

Obscenity, obscenity, "Hurry up!" came from behind me. Just what I needed; a nice, unobtrusive riot.

"Retina, please," the bot said.

I gave the bot a wide-eyed stare while it videofaxed my eyes.

"Drive on around to the loading dock and have a good evening." The smile was back on its face. All was forgiven. I let out a sigh and was thankful that my actions hadn't tripped any programs in the bot to cause it to do a credit check on my card so that it would compare my retina to that of the card's owner. When the banks discovered that the card was stolen, the authorities would be able to find out who had used the card by checking my retina pattern. But that would take a while and I would be long gone by then. Besides, I figured my death had already shot my credit rating to hell.

I eased the van around to the back of the building and stopped. I ordered the bots to place the food in the back of the van carefully. But like typical work bots, they managed to throw the packages of food around despite my instructions. Added to their clumsiness was the fact that they were all made in the form of pink dogs and made a sound like a cross between a bark and a chirp as they worked. As I leaned against the scarred loading dock, I made a mental note never to shop at a Happy Dog store again.

The bikers came around and snarled a bit since I was between them and their order of synthejuana. They quit griping when I stood up to face them for a moment and pulled back my jacket to reveal the Beretta I'd stuffed into my waistband. I put the worst look I could on my face—which wasn't hard since I was downwind of the bikers (most bikers must develop body odor to attract attention). At the sight of the firearm and with a quick mood change, one of the greasers flashed a reasonable imitation of the Happy Dog smile at me. Even bikers can be friendly given the proper motivation.

I didn't hang around to see how long it would last. Life in the Twenty-first Century isn't all it's cracked up to be, I decided as I kicked the last bot out of the way and slammed the cargo door of the van.

I spent the next two hours hitting every store that had any type of supplies I might be needing. Soon my shopping spree had the van pretty well stuffed. My final stop was a hardware store where I picked up some carbonylon rope and got out just before the place was held up.

The store sealed itself up with the criminals, customers, and owner inside its structure to wait until the police finally got around to checking things out. Knowing it could be days before the law arrived, I left the van parked and carefully tied everything down inside so that things wouldn't jostle about if I should have to do a little impromptu flying. While I wasn't anxious to do any flying (not after seeing the World Government's fighters in the air the last time I played birdie), I figured it might allow me to shake a hi-pee if I ran into any trouble on the road.

With the gear stored as securely as I could get it (Boy Scout knots never being one of my fortes—I was always interested in the Girl Scouts), I left the KC dome and its drizzle, which was starting to fall as the moisture from the hot air collected on the dome's cool metallic undersurface to drip down on the city. The dirty drops of rain splattered against the windshield, then suddenly stopped as I left the protection of the dome and was back under the open sky.

As I left the area guarded by the KC police to again head for New Denver, things became wilder and slummier. Finally I was in "Indian Country," in the no-man's land and up on the highway. While the surface of old interstate 70 isn't much worse than when it had been put down in the middle of the last century, traveling the open road is always a scary proposition. At night, it's downright treacherous. The Night Creeps were just as bad as I'd heard.

One plus was the speed I could get out of the van and the new power system I had created. And since there weren't any police eyes—in working condition—on the interstate, and the hi-pees didn't patrol at night because of the danger, I didn't have to worry about attracting undue attention. So I kept the van at an even 100 klicks per hour with occasional peaks of 150 when it looked like it would be good not to stay in an area too long. Any faster and I would probably plow into one of the wrecked vehicles that littered the road; any slower, I chanced getting stopped by the Night Creeps. (And even with my speed, I was forced to clip a couple of them just after I got up on the highway; that's hard on the bodywork of a van.)

The Night Creeps were out in full force. The few new vehicles that I saw on the road had been stopped by the Night Creeps; the stretches of darkness were broken by the red glow of fires along the way as the vehicles were slowly being dismantled and bits of their plastic bodies burned. I didn't see any victims and didn't slow to look. I figured it was everyone for himself for those of us who were crazy enough to be out on the interstate at night. Each of us knew we risked being eaten.

After several hours of dodging and weaving and holding my gun in sweaty fingers from time to time, I was pretty well worn out. And starting to be careless.

I just missed hitting a black truck that was all but invisible to my headlights. It was turned on its side and blocked all of the lane I was in and extended into the shadows of the ditch. I wove around it with a screech of rubber.

As I got up my nerve and speed again and had just started to relax, I discovered that a group of crazies had apparently removed the bridge ahead of me. Or maybe there had been some roadwork the day before. If so, the Night Creeps had removed the warning signs if there had ever been any. All of a sudden, the road ahead of me was gone and my lights showed only an empty expanse between me and the roadway across a large, shadowed chasm.

I didn't feel at all sleepy anymore. Nothing like the prospect of an unexpected plunge into empty space to wake a guy up. And at 100 klicks per hour, things happen quickly.

As the car sped toward the edge of the abyss, I slammed on the brakes. In a long skid, I could see that there was no way I could stop in time. A group of Night Creeps was standing at the side of the road croaking and cheering as I whizzed by.

Words of wisdom formed in my mouth. Repeat your favorite four-letter word five or six times and you'll have the general idea of what I shouted in a very heroic manner as the space between me and the end of the road was quickly eaten up.

Then I realized that I did have one chance: *fly!* Like a bat. At this point, I would have flapped my arms but, fortunately, I had a better idea: "Computer on," I sputtered above the squeal of the rubber.

"Yes."

"Antigrav mode," I said, wishing that I hadn't made a code to keep other people out. The road sounds quit and we were suddenly falling, weightlessly. "Code three . . . uh . . . four . . . six," I gasped with a dry mouth. I pushed the turn signal up—the direction I wanted to go. It started blinking crazily since the antigrav units weren't engaged yet.

The front of the van was now pointing down as I arced through the darkness. The lights showed the ground that was coming up to smash me. All I could hear was the purring of the engine and the sound of the wind whistling outside the van as it plunged downward.

Suddenly, the turn signal stopped blinking; the antigrav units were in operation. I was thrown against the seat harness and felt my eyes trying to bug out of their sockets as the earth continued to rush toward the front of the van.

The computer had been programmed to avoid a crash at all costs—my greatest worry in flying—and it was doing its job. I had to wonder if crashing might not have been more gentle, however, as the seat harness cut into my skin and my eyes continued to head for the ground in the rapid deceleration. A rain of small candies sprinkled onto the inside of the windshield and was followed by a hail of small freeze-dried food containers as a plastic grocery sack behind me gave way. I prepared for some of the larger gear stored in the van to come loose and smash into me from the rear. Fortunately, that didn't happen.

The van righted itself and hurtled back up; my eyes blacked out as the blood left my brain and headed for all points south. I moved the signal to the middle, hover position and my vision came back. I sat there a moment, remembered to breathe, and listened to my hair turn gray. I was in one piece!

As my anger replaced my fear, I was tempted to try out my rifle marksmanship on the Night Creeps I could hear hooting behind me.

It would just be a waste, I decided. There were plenty more to take their places and I had neither the time nor ammunition to spare in venting my anger. Stones were starting to ding off the van, too. I pushed the accelerator down and flew to the other side of the overpass, hovered over the road a moment, and did a 360-degree turn to be sure the area was clear of Night Creeps on the side of the great divide I was on; then I set the vehicle down.

The howls of rage on the other side of the chasm continued. I wiped off my shaking, sweaty palms, and spoke with a quavery voice, "Antigrav off."

"What?" the computer replied.

I cleared my throat, "Antigrav off."

The signal started flashing a left turn (rather than its downward travel sign) and the van settled down with its full weight on the road. I floored the accelerator to put as much distance as I could between me and the things behind me. I wondered how many people they'd catch before sunrise.

It was several hours before I became sleepy again. Fear is a great stimulant. At dawn, I turned off the road and floated the van over a stretch of burned grass and a small gully toward a grove of cottonwoods that glistened in the morning light. There I put the van into a hover at the top of the trees where it would be hidden and out of reach to anyone on foot. As the van was gently rocked by a low-moaning breeze, I reclined my chair and fell asleep.

I awoke to the sound of traffic on the interstate several hours later. The sun shone through the cottonwoods and created patterns of gold and green; the heavy leaves sounded like drops of rain as the wind clapped them against one another.

After opening the door and relieving myself, I brought the van back down and tried to decide—as I ate some Munchies—how to get back to the road without being seen. There was no easy way to do that. I carefully drove over the rough terrain and waited at the gully edge until no traffic was within sight, then shot across the chasm and nearly scraped the far rim in my haste to get across. Settling the van down, I drove on over the sand, up the grade, and pulled onto the road as a road train went thundering by and followed it into New Denver to meet Nikki.

7

When I'd finished my story, Nikki just said, "Antigrav rods? Sure you're feeling all right?"

"Yes . . . *NO!*"

We both laughed.

"It looks like you're my best bet, even though you seem to be a real lightning rod for trouble," Nikki said.

"What?"

"OK, I was already leaving. I'm packed. No doubt whoever's after you will figure you've told me your story—which you have. So now I'm a marked woman. Let me get dressed. I've nothing to lose at this point by going with you." She got up.

"But—"

"No buts. You're the only chance I've got. And quit looking at me like that. This towel is anchored on very securely."

I blushed. It was hard not to stare at a body like Nikki's. I knew better than to try to talk her out of coming with me. She had a mind of her own. And, quite frankly, I was glad to have a partner in my lunacy. I just regretted the danger that I'd managed to get Nikki sucked into.

In a few moments, Nikki returned fully dressed in a tight green jumpsuit. "Come here."

She handed me a men's shirt and unlatched the shirt I had on. "Take off your shirt and see if this fits. It's one of Kraig's. He has dozens squirreled away here."

It fit.

"OK," Nikki said, "we'll pack up a bag for you. Bet you haven't any other clothes, judging from your outfit."

"That bad?"

She nodded. "One more thing. Come in here." She led me into the dressing room. "Since your van's been changed and you were careful coming out here, I have a feeling you got spotted by your pretty face. Maybe they've stationed an agent at each area where you might show up. You need a change of face."

"What?" Then I saw what she had in mind. "Oh, come on, Nikki—"

Before I could do anything she had the instaface kit slapped on me. "Any preference?" she asked.

"Just make me look even more handsome," I muttered through the machine.

She snickered. I felt the synthaskin growing into my face. It felt foreign for a moment then felt like part of me. "Now open your eyes," she said.

"Nikki—"

Too late, I blinked and felt the lens pop onto the surface of my eyes.

"What color of hair?"

"Green."

"OK—"

"No, wait—"

She just laughed.

Fortunately it only became blond. She removed the machine from my face.

"Now your own mother wouldn't recognize you."

I studied my face in the mirrored wall. "My own mother wouldn't want to recognize me."

Nikki changed her own face as well. Neither of us looked a lot different. Just different. And plain. Both of us were blond, which would cause—I hoped—a person's eye to notice our hair rather than our plain faces. Nikki had done a good job. And it would stay that way for at least a couple of weeks until our bodies rejected the synthaskin and it sloughed off our faces.

Fifteen minutes later we sneaked out the building's rear service door with three bags—one filled with Kraig's clothes that had been appropriated for my use, and two of clothing and odds and ends for Nikki. We also had two bundles: one a slightly used needle rifle and the other an industrial laser. Each "tool" was wrapped in a pillowcase. If nothing else, I was picking up quite an arsenal.

No one was on the street. That looked good but might be bad. We waited a moment.

"Stay here," I said. "I'll pick you up in a minute."

"No way," she replied and stepped out onto the street with me. I stood there a moment with two bags and the needle gun and decided it was useless to argue. A bag lady came around the corner a block away and looked at us.

"Come on," I whispered and tugged Nikki in a quick walk to the van. We resisted running like scared rabbits. After enough lifetimes to make a cat feel lucky, we reached the van. We looked back. No one was on the street.

I had seen it in her face the first time I'd mentioned it at the apartment: Nikki wanted to fly the van. So once we were inside, I might just as well have been trying to talk a Seeker out of using his joy circuit. I explained to her again about my experience with the two fighters that had tried to down my flying turkey.

But she refused to take no for an answer. And she had even figured out a safe way to fly without being detected by radar.

And what red-blooded man is going to not give in to anyone as beautiful as Nikki?

What made the flight safe was that the new rockets—which Nikki had been flying as navigator—use powdered aluminum in their fuel to pep up their lift-off. The metal in the rocket's exhaust messes up the radar. It doesn't take an Einstein to figure out the possibilities there.

After stopping near the ruins of what must have once been a large home, we repainted the van (a nice pink—yes, Nikki picked it), changed the van's license imprint, had a picnic, and tried to stay cool during the hot afternoon that's so common in the thin air of the Denver area.

By the time night fell, Nikki knew the vehicle inside and out and had even done some reprogramming of the computers to make the van fly a bit faster and safer.

I hoped.

She was a navigator and knew what she was doing with

the computers, but flying in a vehicle designed to hug the ground is not without its more terrifying—if challenging—aspects. White-knuckle flights are the norm in a flying van.

As the sun set behind the snow-topped, purple mountains, we drove over a worn plastic road to get as close as we could to the rocket port. We parked the van next to the barbed ribbon-wire fence surrounding the field. I used the needle rifle to put out the few flood lights in the area so that no one could see us take off. We waited.

Nikki tried out the controls and took the van up ten meters—still below the ground clutter that would keep us hidden from the radar, then went through a few maneuvers to get the hang of things. My stomach stayed on the ground somewhere below us then jumped into my throat as I heard, in the distance, the crackling sound of rocket engines becoming super-hot. The sound carried through the night as the sky in the direction of the rocket port glowed red.

I sat back in my seat and tried to relax. She knows what she's doing. She knows what she's doing. She knows what she's doing, I told myself.

"Do you know what you're doing?" I asked.

"Relax. Here we go."

We took off at a speed that I hadn't imagined possible. Not blackout acceleration, perhaps, but certainly fast enough to put permanent wrinkles into the side of your skin facing the seat. Nikki had certainly changed the computers' programs. As we rose, Nikki guided the van toward the rocket field and kept the cloud of vapor the rocket was riding on between us and the radar installation of the port.

"Fantastic," she laughed. "Want to follow the rocket a ways?"

"Sure," I said, hoping my voice didn't betray my fear. After a bit, though, I started to get into the spirit of things. The only sound was the wash of the air past the van. Nikki really did know what she was doing. It was fantastic.

"Will we remain hidden?" I asked after a bit.

"Should. Sometimes the radar here in Denver has ghosts anyway. They won't think much of it as long as we're matching speed with the rocket. That isn't hard." She whispered something to the computer and we speeded up a bit more. "Unbelievable," she said.

We arced up with the rocket and followed its plumed path toward the south. The sky above us turned jet black and the stars became sharp points of light; we saw a second sunset, which looked almost like a rainbow framing the mountains down and to the west of us. It became difficult to breathe.

When the rocket's booster dropped on parachutes, we followed it down.

"I'd like to race the rocket, but we'd only have space to inhale at the top of its path," she explained. Her voice sounded thin because of the lack of air in the van. "They leave the atmosphere at the top of their ballistic arc."

We fell back down into nighttime with the booster, dropping in free fall until the wind caught the chutes of the booster so that we could slow our descent. My stomach again felt as if it had made a left turn while the rest of us traveled to the right. Once the free fall had ended, I settled down and enjoyed—as much as possible—the sight of the ocean racing up to meet us.

"We ought to get an altimeter so we can keep from smashing into the ground," Nikki said.

Very reassuring, I thought, and closed my eyes until we finally stopped our fall. The wind whipped the chutes down into the Gulf of Mexico; we hovered over the water just off shore from Texas. We sat watching the twinkling lights from the shore as they danced in the ocean in front of us.

"Won't the radar pick us up?" I asked.

"Yeah. But they won't recognize us as a moving thing. We'll be part of the waves at this height."

The moon came up so that we could see the water clearly in its yellow glow. Nikki pushed the van's accelerator and we hurtled toward the shore, then slowed, skimmed over the beach for several hundred meters, hopped a weedy hedge, and parked under a tall, gnarled palm tree.

After sitting for a few minutes looking out over the ocean, we got out of the van, kicked off our shoes, and walked hand in hand in the gentle surf of the Gulf. The moon rose higher and lit the white sand of the beach as a cool, gentle breeze blew in from the water. Almost an hour later we ended up again in the van. I fell asleep almost instantly in the reclining seat that was beginning to seem like home. (And, no, no romantic goings on—Nikki and I were on a strictly brother-sister relationship. Despite my tries at incest.)

I don't think Nikki slept any that night. She and the two computers whispered and plotted and made lists of things they would be needing.

I wouldn't have slept, either, if I'd known what kind of scheme the three of them were hatching.

8

The late morning sun woke me. In the distance, sea gulls were squawking while the waves added a low hissing rise and fall to the birds' din.

I sat up and looked out over the bright, white sand into the deep blue green that marked the deeper water and splotches of turquoise that were the shallows. Waves formed in the deep water and worked their way to the shore where they sputtered in a roll of hissing, white foam, only to be dragged back from the sand and swallowed up by the next incoming wave.

Nikki abruptly rose up out of the water. Rivulets streamed down her firm, dark arms and thighs as she waded ashore. A pink T-shirt clung tightly to her body in a way that might have been obscene on almost any woman but Nikki. Somehow, her demeanor always made her seem innocent—even though her speech and dress were often otherwise.

After she had dried off and wrapped a towel around her curves, I pushed my eyes back into my head and we had a picnic brunch in the shade of the palm trees around our van. After a polite amount of small talk, Nikki eased into telling me what she and my electronic marvels had been doing the night before.

"Phil," she said around a huge bit of reconstituted dinosteak, "did you ever want to explore space?"

"Sure. And be a cowboy and a fireman and a policeman. Instead, I got a nice calm job where everyone's trying to kill me."

"No, really."

"Sure, I've always wanted to travel into space. Yeah. I even tried to save up money to buy a trip once. And I enjoyed last night's ride—except for not being able to breathe. Why?"

Silence. Nikki seemed to be studying her sandwich.

I should have gotten up and run away right there and maybe drowned myself for good measure. But Nikki is like a flame to a moth. Rather than fleeing, I sat close and proceeded to get burned.

"I was thinking," she said as she munched, "that we could take that van into space if we—"

"Whoa, there. You must be kidding."

"No, really."

"Nikki, there's no way that—"

"Now listen. You've got the power from the flywheel generator to run all kinds of life-support equipment. The van can accelerate with a constant speed. . . . It doesn't need fuel. . . . And the computers can be programmed—in fact are, I took the liberty last night—for Earth orbit. All we need is a couple of suits and some gear. We could—"

"That's crazy. Too dangerous." I popped open a can of soda and wondered if it would be possible to hide in it.

"Phil, things aren't exactly safe here on the ground for us."

"Yeah. But what would we gain in space?"

"That's just it. They'd never think of looking for you on . . . oh, say, the Moon."

"The Moon?" I thought she'd said that a bit too casually. I felt a cold chill dance up and down my spine.

"I did a little figuring and . . ." She launched into her sales pitch.

I was fighting a losing battle from there on out.

And I had always wanted to go into space. It's just that I had never expected to do it in an old van. The more Nikki talked, though, the more enthusiastic I got. Also I had toyed with the idea of a spaceship propelled by the rods when they'd first been perfected; I just hadn't expected to be using a van to travel into space rather than a nice sleek conventional spaceship.

Nikki explained to me that the time was perfect, too. The World Government had, without fanfare, been closing down several of the major Moon bases and was liquidating surplus gear faster than consumers could buy it. All the rocket jocks she'd known had been buying all sorts of hardware and toys. We could probably outfit our expedition for centimes.

She wove her spell the way a spider weaves a web. Before I knew it, I was trapped and we were off in the van to buy some used space suits.

After crashing through the scrubby brush for a while, and making low flights that—I hoped—were off the radar, we finally located a road that led to a highway. I parked the van at the first electro-charge station (hoping the attendant wouldn't become too curious about why the van didn't need to be charged) and found out we were on Galveston Island. Using a map we bought from the attendant, along with the one working phone booth between Mexi-Cal and Canada, we finally found the name of a nearby surplus dealer, which we hoped might lead us to a source of the gear we'd be needing.

Several hours later, and despite the errors on the map, we finally located the surplus store at Hitchcock, west of Galveston.

The store was a huge old barn. Crates and old vehicles littered the area around it. A chain-link fence enclosed the cemetery-like area around the barn where it seemed that all vehicles in the area crawled to when it came time for them to die. With a bit of originality, the owner had painted, in huge amateurish letters, "Space and Military Surplus" over the chipped red paint of the wooden structure.

We stopped in front of the huge eyesore. No other working vehicles were in the customer parking lot. The hot Texas wind pummeled sand against the side of the van.

"Are you sure we want to go in?" I asked.

"Yes!"

"Assuming we find anything of use, what are we going to pay for things with? I chucked my card outside New Denver."

"I've got some jewelry. Barter. Anything else we could trade?"

"I hate to drag a needle gun in—might give the owner a

heart attack. How about your laser? Industrial lasers get
good prices.''

''Sounds good. I have no attachment to it.''

''It ought to get us a lot. *If* we work our trading right.
Let's leave the laser in the van till we see if there's
anything here.'' I had my doubts.

We got out of the van and walked toward the gate. I
squinted at Nikki in the bright sunlight. She looked so
different with her blond hair and the synthaskin; I had to
smile. Nikki didn't look like Nikki anymore.

''What are you smiling at? You look like you know
something I should know about.''

''I was just thinking I liked the way you looked before
you changed your face.''

She laughed, ''I like you better the way you are *now*,''
she gave me a shove as she raced ahead of me toward the
store.

I chased her to the barn door; both of us were giggling
like teenagers as we pulled it open and stepped into the
cool darkness of the interior of the building. Once in, we
got quiet. It was like a museum.

I couldn't believe what all was there. Spotlights, hung
in the ceiling, cut through the gloom with beams that
caught the dust particles in the air and bathed equipment in
light down on the floor. Other piles of machinery sat
hidden in the dark and under dust tarps, looking like large
animals waiting for their prey. The contrast between the
highly lit areas and those in darkness made it necessary to
study what you were looking at before your mind could
make any sense of the jumble.

Large bins holding small parts spread out along one
unpainted wall in a haphazard manner while space suits of
various designs hung down the back of the mammoth room
in a long line, looking like alien soldiers. An ancient space
capsule was suspended from the rafters of the barn and
slowly turned in the cool breeze of an air-conditioning duct
that had recently been bolted to the ceiling. In one dusty
corner, a convention of spacebots stood frozen as if waiting for a command to get to work.

''Help you folks,'' a voice came out of the gloom and
made us both jump.

We turned to see a beefy-looking man with black whiskers shuffle into the light as he came toward us. Dressed in dirty white space overalls with a vintage NASA baseball cap, he bumped and dragged as he moved on a pair of crutches. One leg seemed to be paralyzed and scraped along as he approached. The twisted member looked out of place on his otherwise perfect muscular body.

"We need some gear. Is any of this operational?" I asked.

"Most isn't. Some is. All looks good, though. Unless you're needing it for a project of some sort, you can save a bundle by buying things that are just lookers." He laughed. "Guess I'm talking myself out of some money, here."

"We need equipment that's functional. For . . . experimental work," I said, trying to be as vague as possible. Not that he would believe that we were about to fly to the moon in a van. I just didn't want to tell the truth and have him call the loony bin.

Nikki pulled her list out of the hip pocket of her green coveralls and handed it to him. "We're interested in these. Do you have any of this stuff?"

He took the list, pushed back his cap, and read as he balanced his weight on his crutches. I walked away from him to inspect some of the space suits more closely. Where had I seen his face before? The bum leg suddenly jarred a memory: a supply ship that fell into the moon. One man rescued the survivors in a heroic effort that cost him the use of his leg and later his career. The black beard and athletic frame. Jake Jozek. Big Jake.

Or was it? I walked back to Nikki's side.

He gave us an odd look. "I think I've got most of this. You folks planning on going to Mars or something?"

Obviously he knew his business. Neither Nikki nor I knew what to say.

He went on, "You know, I've been in space. Even on the moon once. You folks have something pretty specific in mind. It's none of my business but—"

"Big Jake Jozek?" I asked, desperately trying to change the subject.

"Yeah," he laughed. "Didn't know anyone still re-

membered. Anyway . . . I think we can work something
out here. Come on back to where I keep the good stuff.''

We followed him as he scraped and dragged himself
across the concrete floor toward a small door at the back of
the barn. ''Didn't know anyone still remembered me,'' he
said. ''They just sent me back, pinned a medal on me, and
that was that. Now, they're dismantling everything. We
should be going to the planets. Now the fools are abandon-
ing the Moon. Just when Earth needs other resources,
they're quitting.'' He turned and smiled, ''Please ignore
the rantings of an old fanatic.''

Nikki and I said nothing. I tried to smile reassuringly so
he wouldn't jack up his prices.

He paused before the door, took out a magnetic key,
unlocked the padlock, and pushed the door open. The
hinges gave a high-pitched squeak that ended in a moan.
He reached into the darkness and flipped on a light.

The door opened into another huge room filled with
more equipment. Unlike the room we had seen, the equipment in this room looked spotless. Several bots glided
about with dust rags as if to demonstrate how carefully the
equipment was being cared for.

''This is my good stuff. No one but the folks that
deliver and unload the gear I buy even know it's back
here. Been saving it for the time when I can buy a rocket—if
and when one becomes available—and make my own way
back into space. Earth's not home anymore. Not with this
leg that holds me back.''

We stood in the doorway a moment then stepped on in.
The equipment was spotless and the area looked more like
a hospital than a storage area. It was obvious that everything had been arranged in an orderly fashion.

''What kind of prices are we looking at for the gear we
need,'' I asked.

He laughed. ''The stuff's not for sale. Whoa there.
Don't give me those long faces. I do have a proposition to
make to you.'' He paused a moment and turned to stand
directly in front of us. ''I can see from that list that you
have something special in mind. You get me back into
space and I'll make it worth your while. Get me to the

Moon with enough gear to get set up in an abandoned base, and I'll supply you with what you need for free.''

Nikki and I stood still, not wanting to betray ourselves. Was this guy on the level?

''Uh, just a minute. We need to have a conference here,'' I pulled Nikki over to one of the spotless corners of the room as a bot scurried out of our way.

''I don't know about this. We should probably get out of here,'' I whispered. ''There's no way we can mount an expedition for all three of us to the Moon. And if he knows—how do we know that he won't turn us in?''

''Why would he turn us in?''

''That's a point. He did get booted out of space. Probably has some real grudges, too.''

''Why not trust him? I bet he's plenty bitter.''

''OK. That's probably right. But I'm not sure if we have enough lifting power to carry all we need. Let alone another—''

''If we accelerate constantly, the trip could be short and—''

''Can you really lift the three of us and some gear?''

''Sure, come on. I'm almost positive that we can do it. And I think we can trust him. We could use a little help from someone who knows what's on the Moon.''

''Well . . . I doubt that we'll find anyone else with this much good equipment. But let's not let him know too much at first.''

Having said that, I spilled my guts. More or less. We didn't tell him *how* we were getting to the moon. Not at first; we didn't want to scare him off. But I did admit that we were going and explained that at least the first trip would be without him until we got the hang of things.

And he insisted that if we had enough lift to get the gear we needed into space and to travel to the Moon, we could take one more hand. He was like the kid that owned the bat and gloves and ball; he was the only game in town.

''I tell you what,'' I said. ''Let me show you what we'll be traveling in and you'll probably want to wait for the second round trip. But you can't tell anyone what you've seen. It could be hazardous.''

Once we'd gained his promise, we drove the van into

the barn. He looked at it and then at us as if we were crazy. I smiled as the little wheels started to move in his head. He tilted his head to listen to the constant whirl of the engine. "What the . . ." He walked around the van. Nikki was driving so I got out.

"Get on in."

He handed me his crutches, backed into the passenger's seat, and pulled himself into place. Nikki flew him around the inside of the barn.

"I can't believe it. I must be dreaming" was all he said when he settled back on the floor and hopped out of the van.

After we were back on the ground, he put a huge CLOSED sign on the front door, locked up, and pitched in and started helping us assemble everything we would be needing. We stopped for a quick lunch and then worked well into the night. About every fifteen minutes Jake would say, "I can't believe it. I must be dreaming."

First we made a big pile of everything we needed, then we started figuring the lift potential as well as trying to figure how to store everything in the van. I could see it was going to be close. At best we'd be like a bunch of soso's stuffed in a package. At worst, Jake would have to stay behind. And I wasn't so sure he would agree to that.

Jake was a big help. He knew a lot of little things that we hadn't thought of that could easily have gotten us killed before we ever even got to the Moon. Things such as the need for a radiant heater as well as a cooling system. And which Moon bases would be easiest for us to settle in without being detected.

By midnight he and Nikki had hammered out the lift potentials and possible rates of acceleration the van could achieve and we'd figured out—more or less—how to fit into the van three people and all the gear they'd need for a short trip through space.

Nikki got the computers out of the van and Jake got a stack of reference books; the two of them sat at the table in the small living quarters Jake had set up in a lean-to on the old barn. They started plotting various orbits that might take us to the Moon. Time after time, they came up with a trip too long for the supplies we could carry or that wouldn't quite get us there. Added to these problems was the fact that the van had to make the first leg of its journey following a rocket flight (to keep us from being detected) even though the van was capable of nearly constant acceleration/deceleration unlike a rocket.

I sat at the table awhile and then quietly sneaked out when I realized that I was in over my head. I reentered the barn and studied the van, which was in the center of one of the bright spots. It looked like an exhibit in a museum. It certainly didn't look like a space craft. If I had had to choose between it and the cow that jumped over the moon, I would have chosen the cow. The van looked like the most unlikely of candidates to get us into space. The proverbial mind boggler.

I also felt . . . jealous. Seeing Jake and Nikki hitting it off together didn't seem to go over well with me. Mentally, I didn't see anything to be jealous about. Emotionally, I felt jealous. Unfortunately, the heart wins out over the brain when it comes to feelings. So I moped around in the shadows of the barn. Finally, I started exploring and ended up in the hayloft. There I opened an old wooden door and stood staring at the Moon, not quite full tonight, which was coming up in the east.

"There you are."

I turned to see Nikki coming up the ladder.

"What are you doing?" she asked.

"Baying at the Moon," I said.

Nikki looked at the Moon a moment. "It's hard to believe. But I think we've figured out a way to really do it. The figures are there and we have the vehicle. All we have to do is go." She looked at my face. "You look sad."

"Yeah. Well, I guess it's a little bit of a letdown, somehow. Part of me is excited and part of me would like to be sitting in a soft chair watching the 3V."

"Even if bag ladies try to zap you?"

"Maybe we could skip that part. Come on, it's my dream. Don't throw in your bag ladies."

Silence for a bit longer. Nikki reached out and gave my hand a squeeze. "Listen, Phil. I know that. . . . Well, don't rush things. It's going to be a while before I get over

Kraig. He may be a mess, but he was my mess. All I ever had. Give me time.''

I wasn't sure I understood. But enough to go on. She gave me a quick kiss on the cheek and pulled me toward the ladder. ''Come on, Phil. Jake's so charged up he'll start flying around the room if there isn't someone to keep him grounded.''

We spent the next few hours listening to Jake spin his tales about his time in space and on the Moon. As he told his stories, a bond was woven that held three dreamers who were hoping to claim a chunk of the Moon for themselves.

9

The next morning, Nikki and I slept late. Jake was up welding an extra storage bay to the top of the van. It looked like the dickens but gave us the extra space we needed. By the time things were rounded up and we were ready to go, the day was half gone. Jake's nephew, Mark, had arrived and was to take over the business while Jake was "out of town" as he put it. Nikki left her jewelry and the industrial laser for Mark to sell if he needed cash to pay Jake's bills. Jake didn't want Mark to sell any of his surplus gear until we'd returned and had a better idea of what we'd be needing.

We drove the van back out into the hot Texas sunlight and waited for Jake to get in. He jumped into the old business chair that he'd welded just behind the two front seats of the van. I hoped his welds were good. I could just imagine him flying about inside the van at some critical moment.

We made our way through the slums of Galveston and up to Highway 45, which led directly to the Houston rocket port. Because of the poor condition of the road and the number of vehicles that had been abandoned on it, we didn't reach our destination until nightfall. Fortunately the rioting going on in Texas City had diverted the hi-pees into that area; we were free to fire at highwaymen and weren't stopped as we slowly made our way toward Houston.

Arriving at dusk was perfect for our plans since we were going to follow a rocket into space, again under the cover of the night. Once in space, we'd alter our course and then depart for the Moon. While we wouldn't remain hidden from radar detection once the rocket started its arc back to its destination halfway around the world, there would be little chance of being seen, and if we were located the fact that our speed and directional changes would be so different from those of conventional spacecraft would probably make an Earthside watcher think we were a gremlin rather than an actual spacecraft. Also, we'd be headed out so that, even if they wanted to, it would be impossible to intercept us.

In the dark, Jake let most of the air out of the van's tires so they didn't pop when we got into space. Then the three of us slipped into our space suits and connected them into the support system powered by the car's generator. We left our helmets off so that we could talk freely.

Jake sat behind us, Nikki was in the passenger seat, and I sat behind the wheel of my van. Jake's head somehow looked ridiculous without his NASA cap.

"According to the schedule we picked up, the Paris-bound rocket should be launched in a couple of minutes," Nikki said.

"Yeah. Everyone get buckled up," I said.

Jake reached forward and gave my hand a shake that threatened to crack some bones, "Good luck, Captain Hunter."

"Where'd you get this 'Captain' stuff? 'Major Hunter.' " Nikki and Jake laughed.

Nikki leaned back and gave him a quick kiss. Now I really felt jealous.

I lifted the van off the pavement and floated over the fence and onto the rocket field. The force of the antigrav rods pushing downward caused the fence to sag nearly to the ground. It looked as if an elephant had crawled over it.

Right on schedule, the nighttime sky glowed red and I waited for Nikki to doublecheck to be sure we were following the right rocket. She studied the computer-radar tie-in that we'd improvised from Jake's surplus equipment while the surplus radio picked up transmissions from the port and made a garbled sound that Nikki seemed to be able to decipher.

"That's it. Here we go," she said.

I hit the Auto button on the dash and leaned back, hoping that the computer would follow the radar blip of the rocket rather than a flock of gulls. One malfunction was all we needed to have a major catastrophe. After vowing never to ride a machine-controlled rocket, I was now hurtling through the atmosphere chasing a rocket controlled by a machine in a van controlled by a computer. I whispered a silent prayer to ask forgiveness for my stupidity.

I also wished that we'd gotten a couple of parachutes from Jake.

"Phil."

"Uh."

"Your helmet. Or are you planning on holding your breath for the round trip."

The choice wasn't hard to make. I got my helmet off the floor and turned it the proper direction.

"Phil, just a minute."

As I turned to look, Nikki leaned over and gave me a long, passionate kiss, then pulled on her bubble helmet before I had time to try for a second one. I wished I could see her face in the dark van; all that showed on her mirrored helmet was the reflection of the lights from the dash panel and the various odds and ends of instrument lights on the equipment we'd added to the van. Nikki was an enigma wrapped in a space suit.

Jake gave a long yelp for joy, which threatened to ruin our suits' communications gear, as we started our journey toward the Moon. And after Nikki's kiss, I felt like I could have flown to the Moon without the van.

10

Although we were hurtling around the Earth at an enormous speed, the blue and white globe below us looked like it was only slowly meandering by while we hung in space. We had followed the passenger rocket up through the atmosphere and then passed it from a distance as it stopped its acceleration and started its downward descent back toward the ground. We continued to accelerate and headed on around the Earth to pick up more speed for our jump across space into the gravity field of the Moon.

The sun soon sank behind us and we spiraled back over the nighttime sky, into Earth's cold shadow and outward, toward the Moon.

We did little during our flight. We sat and talked, tried to get the pastey food through the intake port of our suits (Jake was the only one who was very successful at this), and tried to discreetly use the waste disposal system in the suits with a minimum of fuss. (After spilling water down my neck and nearly dropping a pint of urine on the floor of the van, I was not too impressed with the freedom enjoyed by the glamorous astronauts of the 3V shows. Nothing like a plastic sack of excreta sitting in a pouch on your suit to take the romance out of things.)

We didn't suffer from having to be weightless. Nikki and Jake had plotted our course with an eye toward maximum speed since we didn't have to worry about expending motivating energy. Because of this, we had almost constant "gravity" as the van pushed ahead and our bodies tried to stay behind. About the only time we were weight-

less was for the few moments when the computer maneu-
vered the van about—so we wouldn't feel like we were
hanging on our heads—to start pushing against the Moon's
gravity as the lunar gravity overcame that of the Earth. I
was thankful for the lack of weightlessness; after the few
moments of weightlessness there was little doubt in my
mind that I would have suffered from space sickness while
Nikki and Jake sat beside me perfectly blissful of my
sufferings. Whining about stomach ailments is not a good
way to impress an attractive member of the opposite sex or
an old space jock.

About the only major problem was cramped muscles;
you can't just stop and step out to stretch when you're
hurtling through space.

During the first few hours of our flight, Nikki was quite
busy with an electronic astrolabe and a computer file that
gave us the correct coordinates we needed. After a while
she became convinced that the computer was doing a
perfect job of flying us and only made an occasional
sighting for my peace of mind. (And once she didn't even
bother to turn the astrolabe on—talk about trying to soothe
the pilot's nerves. Nikki knew all the navigator tricks, I
could tell.)

We orbited the Moon one time to allow the computer to
adjust our speed and then located our first destination. Our
whole trip took less than one day—considerably less than
the three days taken by conventional rocket flights to the
moon.

Our computer dropped us quite close to the airless surface of the Moon; I tried not to scream as we dropped
through space. We skimmed across the barren, pock-marked
gray land and, after the computer made one last stomach-
wrenching adjustment and sounded a warning beep in our
helmets, we were hanging over the Copernicus Mining
Base a little off the equator of the Moon in the Carpathian
Mountain range between the Oceanus Procellarum and the
Mare Imbrium and to the east of Kepler crater.

The computer had flown us flawlessly to our destination
on the Moon.

"Well, you and Jake did a perfect job in calculating and
programming our flight."

Jake gave a grunt that a frog would have recognized as meaning "thanks."

Nikki, a bit more conventional, spoke English, "Thanks. It's nice to have a new type of problem for a change. I'm afraid rocket-flight navigation made me a little rusty at figuring orbits. Ready to go down?"

"Yeah. Now or never, right? I hope I can do as well as you guys did in programming the computer." I wiped my hands against my legs, even though the sweat remained on my palms thanks to the fact that they were wrapped in heavy space gloves. "Ready?"

"Take her down, Captain," Jake's voice said in my helmet's speaker.

I flipped the turn signal out of its hover position and we slowly fell downward. Though there was really nothing to worry about, it seemed a bit anticlimactic after the long computerized trip to get to where we were going with a flip of a turn signal. Hardly first class. I decided to have Jake get us some flashing lights to wire into the van before we took anyone we really wanted to impress on a flight.

The mining base was dwarfed by the sheer size of the Copernicus crater. The one-sixth gravity of the Moon made for spectacular contrasts of heights with the scraggly, un-weathered crater walls jutting up unlike any mountain range on Earth. Because of the greater curvature of the Moon, the far side of the crater walls dropped almost out of sight as we neared the rough floor where a giant meteor had fallen onto the Moon before mankind had even started chipping away at flint knives.

The rocket sled ramp soon came into sight and the artificial smoothness of man's handiwork showed on the rock around it. The ramp stretched down toward the base, which was nestled in the northern end of the crater. Though the sled had been designed to launch the metal ingots mined and processed on the Moon, Jake said that the base had been closed just before it had gotten ready for auto-mated production. And the question none of us could answer sprang up to puzzle me again. Why had the base been closed down? Earth needed the resources. The best guess among the three of us was that the powers-that-be on

Earth just couldn't make enough money at it. Perhaps it was easier to let people on Earth starve. Who knew?

After an eternity, we reached the floor of the crater and I carefully steered the van over to land on the smooth field built for supply rockets. It was nestled among huge boulders that jutted from the lunar dust that had filtered in around them. Beside it was the small solar-powered beacon that had allowed our computer to home in on the base. A slight jolt marked the end of our descent. I looked over at Nikki.

"We made it." I could barely see a smile on her face inside the mirrored bubble helmet.

"Yes. We're really here."

Then it sank in as Jake yelled, "We're here!"

I jumped when he yelled and would have bumped my head if my seat belt hadn't held me down.

"How about a little stroll?" Nikki asked unfastening her seat belt, soundlessly since there was no air in the van.

"Don't mind if we do," I unbuckled my harness and popped open the door of the van. I sat a moment and looked at the Earth, which was the one splotch of color in the gray and black lunar landscape. Then I studied the ground and tossed myself from the van with what I had aimed to be the proverbial "one small step." I banged the back of my helmet on the van roof, fell out the door, bounced off the dust, somersaulted, and landed on shaky legs. Lucky for me there were no sharp rocks around and the lunar gravity is not too great. Nikki hadn't seen my acrobatics so I tried to act as if nothing had happened.

"Everything OK?" Jake asked.

"Sure," I said, hoping my panic didn't show in my voice. I wasn't in such a great hurry after that.

Needless to say, the weak lunar gravity takes some getting used to. It's rather like walking in chest-deep water without the resistance of the water to hold you back. A gentle jump can bounce you four or five feet into the airless "air." By the time we'd gone the short distance across the plain separating us from the base's entrance, both Nikki and I had pretty well mastered the kangaroo hop that can get you around so quickly on the Moon. Jake's suit had the legs tied together and he functioned as if he'd been born on the Moon; his hopping motions were both graceful and functional.

I half expected the base to be locked up. But of course it wasn't. There aren't many unaccounted-for persons walking around on the Moon. The main problem was whether or not the air locks would be operational.

Jake rotated the heavy ring on the door and it popped open. We found ourselves in a white plastic air lock big enough for eight or nine people at the most. We stepped into the small room. I closed and twisted the lever of the door behind us; sunlight came through the translucent plastic so that we could see. Nikki pushed the cycle button. Nothing happened. The lock wasn't functional.

"Power's down," Jake said. "The air locks all have an emergency switch in them so that it's impossible to accidentally get locked out."

"What's it look like?"

"Probably a panel. Small metal plate door. Something like that."

We searched around, carefully checking the ceiling, walls, and floor. Finally, I spotted the thin lines of a panel cover. For some reason it was designed to blend into the rest of one of the walls; it made everything look nicer but was a very poor practice for such a critical device. "Is this it?"

"Must be. Can you get it open?"

Getting a hold on a hairline opening is impossible in a space suit. "Remind me to grow fingernails on my gloves next time we come to the Moon."

"Here." Jake handed me a small-bladed screwdriver from the tool kit that he'd mounted on his suit.

I put the blade into the crack and jimmied the plastic apart. It suddenly popped off and the plate went cartwheeling through the space in the chamber, silently bounced off a wall, and slowly fell to the floor. Getting used to the low gravity and airlessness was going to take some time, I decided as I handed the tool back to Jake.

There was one red button under the panel.

"Hey, they don't have auto-destruct buttons on these bases, do they?" I asked.

Nikki laughed, "I know a good way to see if that's it."

"Cross your fingers," I pressed it, hoping we were only kidding. An electric overhead light came on in the chamber to augment the small amount of light coming through the plastic walls.

"OK. Try the cycle button again," Jake said.

Nikki pressed the button and in a moment a low hiss began, gradually growing louder. Our suits quit acting like balloons, and the chamber filled with air.

I cautiously cracked my helmet off the suit as Nikki and Jake removed theirs and unlatched the inner door of the chamber to create a small pop as the pressure differences between rooms evened out. I took a deep breath; stale, recycled, but still air. And after the humid conditions on the inside of the suits, it felt very refreshing, cool, and dry.

We stepped into the first room behind the lock, carefully sealing the door behind us. It was a larger version of the air lock: a huge, white bubble that filtered sunlight through it so that the interior was dimly lit. The electric lights seemed to be off. Flipping the switch beside the door didn't do anything. The power was off inside the base. Fortunately, with a lunar day of fourteen and a half Earth days, we still had several more "days" of light and there was no big hurry to get things started up.

We put our helmets on a small dispatcher's desk sitting next to the door. Nikki and I followed Jake's lead and took off our gloves and laid them beside our helmets.

"Now let's see how this station is set up," I said. "Our first task will be to locate the radio link." Jake had told us that the station sensors were connected to an automatic radio link to Earth. If we didn't disconnect it, it would eventually send back enough information on changes within the base, power systems in use, et cetera, to alert someone on Earth that something was going on in the station. We'd decided that if it suddenly stopped its transmission, monitors on Earth would assume that it was just an equipment malfunction; this was better than having detectors in the base showing that it was occupied (even if those on Earth would be at a loss to explain by whom or what).

The airlock opened into the command center of the base. A quick search allowed us to locate the monitor.

"Say good-night," I said as I jerked the electric cable from its back. To be on the safe side, Jake also disconnected the antenna from the back of the transmitter.

Further exploration of the base showed that it had been abandoned in a hurry. There was enough food and water to supply us for at least a year. There were two problems: the hydroponics area had been shut down (with all the now dead plants in place) and though the mine was ready to be worked, there were no bots in the whole base to start the operation.

The hydroponics situation wasn't too much of a hardship. We used little air and the base had a stock of seeds. It meant that we'd have to clean the growing trays but that could be done during our leisure.

The lack of bots to help set up the mining operation was a major problem, however. The main reason for our landing at the base had been to produce metal from the ore deposited by the impact of the ancient giant meteor that had created the Copernicus crater. The same metal that— with the help of the solar panel's energy and some other odds and ends of equipment that could be scrounged up or even dragged up from Earth—could then be converted into antigravity rods.

But there were no bots to do the work. Apparently the last shipment to make the base operational had been aborted. We'd have to find the bots before it would be possible to carry out our dream.

After a quick meal of instarations, we were ready to call it a day. We made our way to the crew quarters, which extended down into the lunar rock. There were forty cabins down a long underground hallway leading from the command center. Each cabin was large, ten by twenty meters, and contained a pair of bunk beds, desks, two retrieval monitors, a 3V set, and a small bath. Each was also a jumble as the tenants had apparently been forced to sort hurriedly through their belongings to try to decide what to take back to Earth. A few rooms had even ripened as dirty clothing had been left behind to take on a life of its own. But most also had the towels, soap, and other supplies we'd be needing.

Despite my dream of sharing a bed with Nikki, she

picked out a room of her own. I said my good-nights to Jake and Nikki—I was ready to sleep. I heard Nikki laughing out in the hallway; apparently she and Jake had decided to stay up awhile. Was Nikki interested in Jake? I didn't know, but I was too tired to worry about it. The weak lunar gravity made the thin mattress softer than anything on Earth. That—coupled with my exhaustion— made me drop off into a dreamless sleep.

11

"Rise and shine," Nikki said, and I felt a tug on my nose. I opened my right eye to see what was going on and was greeted by the overhead light she'd flipped on. "We need to get going if we're going to get things done today," Nikki said as she left the room.

"Oh, boy . . ." With a brown taste in my mouth, I all but fell from bed then staggered a moment trying to get my footing in the light gravity. I finally made it into the bathroom where a shower of hot, slowly falling water got my eyes to where they'd stay open.

After rifling through the closets in my room, I discovered a pair of yellow coveralls that more or less fit. A pair of slip-on sneakers—which I hoped hadn't been owned by someone with a fungus disease—completed my borrowed outfit. I wondered why I hadn't had the good sense to bring a container of caffinex—which I'd found in the instant-hot packages that filled the storage area of the mess hall—back to my room the night before. On the other hand, thinking about getting out of the room and getting some caffinex gave me the will to live.

I bounced into the control room on my way to the mess. I was surprised to see that the whole front of the room opposite the air lock was now a clear plastic window facing the panorama of the plain formed by the crater bottom. The gray stillness of it seemed alien when viewed from inside the safe confines of the room. Quiet, unfriendly, and lifeless. The pink van sitting in the distance looked like some sort of advertising joke that a used-car dealer might pull. The pink was the only splotch of color on the whole plain.

Jake sat at a console speaking to a computer in a low tone and occasionally punching at a key with a beefy finger.

"How'd you do that?" I asked.

"What?" He turned toward me.

"How'd you get the view?"

"Plastic. When a current goes through it, it becomes transparent. Instant windows. Just had to throw the right switch. We're using so little energy right now that the solar cells show a full charge in the base's storage batteries. We've got power to waste," Jake said with a smile. He went back to his work.

I'd heard about the new plastic but never seen any of it in use. Nikki sat with another computer across her lap and waved as I went through to the mess. I half floated through the mess to the food storage room and hunted up a packet of caffinex. I had to wake up. I popped the seal on it and breathed in the fumes of the brew a moment before drinking, then shuffled back into the control room, trying to get the liquid out of the cup and into my mouth rather than having the caffinex wiggle around in the weak gravity and depart for parts unknown.

"What's on the agenda for today?"

"Good question," Nikki said. "We'd better have a council of war."

"Jake?" I asked.

"Yeah. Uh . . . just a moment." He spoke one last command and the printer next to the computer started coughing out figures. He rose and hopped over to us. I noticed that he'd tied his shoelaces together to allow his good leg to pull his bad one along. He bounced as if he were on a pogo stick.

"Since sleeping all day seems not to be an option," I said, looking at Nikki who looked innocent as usual, "we need to decide what we're going to do. Need to get organized," I said. "Have you two been able to pull anything of interest out of the computers?"

"Yeah," Jake said. "Got a list of mining equipment and set-up procedures from the computer bank before you woke up. We can go over it later, but it looks like we have all the stuff we'd need to keep the base operating and complete the mining operation. Almost. Everything but the bots. It's just a matter of getting the thing up and running, but we can't do it without the bots.''

"Nikki?"

"Yeah. It was among the last of the transmissions they received here before closing up the base. Here's the one line of interest: 'Your industrial bots have arrived—Eratosthenes Base.' ''

"Where in the world—excuse me—where in the Moon is the Eratosthenes Base?" I was having trouble making conversation; I kept looking at Nikki's figure that was temptingly displayed in a tight yellow jumpsuit, unzipped to "see level." Was this noticeably tempting display for my benefit or Jake's?

"Eratosthenes crater is just a hop and a skip from here," Jake said. "The van would get us there in a couple of hours at the most."

"Would they leave the bots behind?" Nikki asked.

"Probably. Bots, even those for mining operations, aren't as expensive as shipping them home. I suspect that the Eratosthenes Base will be like this one. About all they'll have taken out is the crew."

"Do we know that the Eratosthenes Base is closed?" I asked. I could imagine stumbling into the base and then having to hightail it out again.

"I don't have the inside information," Jake said, "but based on the amount of surplus gear that's been hitting the market, I'm willing to bet that none of the lunar bases are in operation."

Nikki spoke, "That certainly fits in with what I heard before I lost my job. The gossip among the rocket jocks was that the Moon had been abandoned."

"So," Jake said, "*if* we could sneak into the base, and get some bots, we'd be able to get the hydroponics started—"

"And then," I continued, "get the metallurgical plant and mining operation ready to go. I'd like to see if it's practical to manufacture the antigrav rods."

"Jeeze," Jake said. "If we could do that . . .''

"*If*," I said. "Building the magnetic furnace and other equipment needed to make the rods won't be easy."

"But if you could," Nikki said. "And then mount a full-scale mining and manufacturing operation if it all looked practical . . ."

"The sky's the limit."

We all thought about it for a moment.

"There are a lot of ifs in all this," I said.

"But we have to have the bots," Nikki said.

"We've nothing to lose," I said. "Any problem with going over right now to check it out?"

There wasn't.

I met Nikki and Jake at the front air lock. Jake had some spare oxygen tanks and a carbonylon cable wound around his suit. "We'd better replace our suit tanks. Most of the tanks in the van are depleted."

Jake and I crunched helmets together trying to help Nikki. While we struggled trying not to look too clumsy she slipped off her own tank and replaced it. When we'd gotten all sorted out, we refilled the empty tanks off our suits and took them with us.

The surface of the Moon is hard to become accustomed to. The Earth is always in the sky. A different side of it, maybe, but always there. Though the sun was setting, it, too, seemed eternally rooted in place. To an Earther, the scene was totally unreal after living on a planet where *all* the heavenly bodies rose and set in twelve hours. It made it seem as if time had stopped for everyone but us as we bounced across the Moon.

We unloaded everything from the van we wouldn't be needing for our short flight so that we'd have more room for transporting bots or other equipment back from the base, if it was actually abandoned. Our raiding party was banking on the ifs. We'd get what we needed *if* Jake was right and Eratosthenes was abandoned and *if* the equipment hadn't been transported back to Earth.

Unloading the van was quite a task. We'd really wedged a lot of stuff into it. It was a half hour before we lifted off and started traveling back up and out of our huge crater. I headed the van toward the northeast and the computer took over as it picked up the homing beam from the Eratosthenes

Base. It was another white-knuckle flight since Nikki had programmed the computer for maximum speed while Jake and I had finished unloading the van.

Maximum speed on the Moon is very fast since you don't have atmosphere for resistance and you're keeping your craft as close as is practical to the surface to minimize the chances of radar detection. Especially when the surface you're traveling over is comprised of lunar mountains—with their sheer grades—the size of those in the Carpathian range. We accelerated the first half of the trip and then decelerated the last half. The tops of boulders and mountains went whizzing by pretty close to our feet. It was fortunate that the suits had gloves so the others couldn't see how tightly I gripped the nonfunctioning steering wheel from time to time.

12

As we neared the Eratosthenes crater, which contained the Eratosthenes Base, we came to a stop and sneaked up on the complex from behind. We kept low and used the mountainlike hills of the area to screen our approach. As we got within several kilometers of the base and had dropped over the crater rim, we hid behind any boulders that were large enough to conceal a floating van. When we had flown to within a couple hundred meters of the base, it became obvious that something was very wrong.

A large crack could be seen from above the dome of the control room. Bits of paper and other garbage lay in the dust in a line coming out from the crack, which had apparently been blown out of the dome when it had developed the split. A sudden loss of pressure had caused the air to push things out as it escaped through the crack.

There were also areas of melted plastic down one side of the dome covering the mining shaft. An industrial laser had apparently been used as a weapon or something. The plastic created a pattern of reversed letters on the wall. Inside they would read KF. Why had they been written from inside? None of us could think of any code or words that had any important meaning. KF? And why would anyone do such a dangerous thing? They were lucky they hadn't punched a hole in the mining dome.

I circled the base slowly before landing. Everything looked quiet.

"What do you think? Shall we land?" I asked. "I'm not too keen on meeting a crazy with an industrial laser." I remembered what had happened the last time I'd seen an industrial laser fired. Having my smiling head sitting out in the lunar dust didn't seem too appealing.

"Nothing seems to be going on now," Nikki said. "Nothing's lit up."

"Let's land and sit a minute. See if anything happens," Jake said.

If someone carves the van into little pieces, we'll figure something's wrong, I thought, as we settled down in front of the main airlock of the base.

"We can't stay too long. We don't have much spare oxygen," Nikki said. We'd hoped to pick up spares in the base.

We sat for ten minutes. Nothing happened.

"I'm going to take a look," I said. I was tired of waiting for a disaster to happen; it was more nerve-racking than doing something. I popped open the glove compartment of the van and pulled out my Beretta.

"Will that work without air?" Nikki asked.

"Yeah. The firing pressure is hundreds of times higher than Earth's air pressure. The loss of the sixteen pounds of air pressure outside won't be a strain on it. Jake, why don't you grab the needle rifle? Nikki, you take the wheel of the van in case we need to make a fast run for it."

Jake and I got out of the van.

"Let's split up," Jake said. "You head for that boulder next to the airlock and I'll cover you."

"OK. Ready?"

Jake steadied himself against the van and aimed at the entrance of the base. "OK, go."

I hippety-hopped toward the boulder like a scared rabbit. When I got behind the boulder and caught my breath, I aimed my pistol at the entrance. "Looks quiet. Come on."

Jake came bounding across the plain like a kangaroo and stopped by the door and waited a moment. "OK. Come on up, Phil."

I bounced toward the door and stopped on the other side of it by plowing into the side of the dome. We waited a moment.

"See anything, Nikki?" Jake asked.

"Looks clear from back here."

"Just a minute, watch the door." I crawled over to the crack in the dome and looked into it and tried to see in the darkness inside. There didn't seem to be anything moving. "The place is a mess. A lot of the communications gear is smashed." I moved to the other side of the crack and checked out the rest of the room. "Someone really trashed it in there. No one's in sight. No bodies either. The crack's just a little too narrow to get through. Has pretty sharp edges."

"That stuff's too tough to break or pry open, too. Let's use the door," Jake said.

Wish I'd thought of that, I thought, as I hopped back to the door. Jake opened up the outer door, peeked in, then motioned and we both went in.

"We have a problem, now," Jake said. "The inner door's made so it can't be opened without cycling air into the air lock. That's normally a nice safety feature; now it's bad since the dome doesn't have air in it."

"Maybe the system is out of air," I said.

"Yeah. Could be. Let's try." He pushed the cycle button. The door closed behind us and the chamber filled with air.

"Damn," Jake said. "We shouldn't open the inner door with the pressure up. It's pretty dangerous. Might rip our suits open if it pulled us in."

"Stand back," I said. I aimed my Beretta at the wall leading out to the plain. "Is this a good spot? No hidden wiring or anything?"

"Good as any. Stay away from the hole when you've made it. It'll create some real suction at first."

I pulled the trigger. The discharge exploded loudly in the air-filled chamber and a small hole appeared in the wall. The air hissed out slowly as our suits ballooned back up.

Then the suits dropped back against our skin as air rushed into the chamber with a steady hiss.

"Forgot about the auto cycle," Jake said. "Let's see if we can turn off the power. Don't get against the bullet hole!"

I was glad he cautioned me since I about put my posterior end against it. Having the seat ripped off your pants in a vacuum can be more than embarrassing. I hated the idea of getting a little ''behind'' into my work, as it were.

Jake pulled off the metal plate on the emergency button, which was located in the same place as the one at our base. He punched it and the air again ran out of the chamber and our suits inflated.

''What are you guys doing in there?'' Nikki asked.

''Don't worry,'' I said. ''Just a little problem getting through the air lock. We're about ready now.''

Jake twisted the door release open and pushed the door ajar, then jumped through it. I followed his example and jumped in, falling on my back with a curse.

Nikki said, ''Hey, are you guys OK?''

''Blasted lunar gravity,'' I said picking myself up. I looked around to be sure it was safe, then straightened up. ''Looks clear. Let's give everything the once over. Don't get sidetracked looking at the damage.''

It was hard not to look. The equipment had apparently been smashed by a crowbar that was sitting on one of the control consoles. Spray paint had been used to write four-letter words as well as a lot of gibberish on the white walls of the control room. A madman seemed to have been in charge of the area.

We moved into the crew quarters. Several were completely gutted by what appeared to have been a flash fire. The hydroponics area was sealed off with air pressure having apparently been maintained in it. We looked through the clear door panel and could see that all the plants inside were dead.

We continued through the complex. I held my pistol ready, wondering who or what might be waiting for us. In the mess hall, things appeared normal. The pantry storage area was full of food just as the one at our base had been. The water tanks were full as well.

The mining area was a disaster. An industrial laser had been left on for some time and had created a pool of molten metal and rock where its beam had been shining. How long it had been on was hard to tell, but its tube was black, indicating that it was worn out. ''Look at that,'' Jake said pointing to the frozen metal pool.

The mining operation itself had never been started.

We moved back into the command room.

"Nikki, how's it look out there?" I asked.

"All's quiet."

"We haven't found anyone in here," I said. "Why don't you come on in? Uh . . . do you have the key to the van? Why don't you lock up?"

"Will do. I'm coming in—don't shoot."

In a few moments, Nikki came through the doorway. "Looks like you guys could use a good house bot."

"Which brings up an interesting point. Where're the bots?" I asked.

"They said in storage bin eight, didn't they," Jake asked. "Let's see." He bounced over to the wall of the command center and pulled a blueprint out of its wall compartment. I moved up alongside him to study the map.

He continued, "Unlike our base, this one was, I think, to serve as a warehouse for the others. See—here's where the storage complex was to be built. Most of it isn't there yet. We didn't see anything. No, wait; see the dotted lines? It's underground. The entrance is . . . there," he pointed to a small circle that led to the massive storage area. "I think I noticed a small dome outside; didn't recognize what it was."

"Makes sense since they'd be loading things up outside. And they wouldn't want to waste air on it either."

Nikki's voice sputtered over our headphones, "Hey!"

Both Jake and I spun around with our weapons ready.

"Hold your fire," Nikki said. She pointed to the computer that she had turned on. "Just found the last entry in the log. Apparently the going-home party got a little out of hand with some synthadrugs that the crew had made, or brought with them. The crew got pretty frantic . . . KF probably belongs to one Kerry Franklin, who was taken out in chains. . . . Uh . . . the last entry is 'Base abandoned, Tuesday, March—' "

"All right!" Jake said. "Oficially abandoned. No one will be coming back."

"Now if the bots are still in storage. Anything about that?"

"Uh . . . no. Nothing."

Jake was again looking at the blueprint of the base. "It's got to be that little dome we saw off to the side of us when we dropped in."

"Bet so, let's go out and see. Nikki, want to come along?"

"You better believe it. This place gives me compression blood."

13

From the ground, it was pretty obvious that a lot of equipment must have been transferred from cargo rockets to the underground storage area. The dust showed the trampling of hundreds of feet and claws where men and bots had worked to carry heavy burdens into the warehouse. A few vehicle tracks criss-crossed the trail that stretched from the large landing port over to the small dome marking the entrance to the underground storage area. The tracks looked like they'd just been made; the lack of atmosphere meant that the prints could remain as they were for centuries unless someone disturbed them.

The white plastic dome over the storage entrance was mostly door. When we released it, it parted along three seams and spread open so that it looked like some type of mechanical bird getting ready to take off.

"Why didn't they just store everything on the surface?" I asked.

"Earther mentality maybe," Jake said. "You see it all the time in space. We've all grown up with the ravages of the atmosphere. There're some other reasons, too, though. The temperature's more constant a few feet into the surface and there's less damage to equipment during a solar flare-up."

"Solar flare-up! I'd forgotten about that," I said. "How do we know we're not being fried right now?"

"See the panel right here on the wrist of your suit?" Jake pointed to his wrist then switched on his suit lights and bounded down the ramp leading into the cavernous storage chamber with one leap. "If it turns black, you head for shelter."

"What shelter?" I asked as Nikki and I followed him into the cavern.

"That's the other reason," Jake said. "The lunar rock gives shielding from radiation. Same reason the crew quarters and mess hall are underground."

I reminded myself to check my wrist indicator every five minutes.

As we reached the bottom of the ramp, we had to turn around to bathe the area in our suit lights. Straight ahead from the base of the ramp were a number of lunar rovers—large tracked vehicles that were useful only for traveling around on the surface of the crater since they couldn't climb the steep incline of the crater walls. Next to the rovers were three little platforms with a rail around two seats.

"What are those?" I asked.

Jake turned to see where I was pointing. "Those are two-man flitters. They use them for short trips around the cavern. They have a very limited carry capacity." He laughed. "When we get other vehicles built with gravity rods in them, they'll really simplify moving things on the Moon."

"And Earth," Nikki added.

"Yeah, we'll really cause a revolution in the way things are done."

Extending down to the right of the ramp were six empty rooms. To the left were rooms of boxes.

"What are in those boxes?" Nikki asked and sprang toward them. She looked at them in her light then hopped over to some more. "Rats, they're bar coded—it's impossible to tell what's in them. We'll have to look for the computer manifest. Gee, there must be enough stuff to outfit a whole tribe of people," she said, looking at the rows of boxes that extended beyond the reach of our lights.

"Let's go back the other way," I said. "The bots would be in larger containers. These are all too small."

We located the bots in a huge chamber that, like the others, had been carved out of the solid rock. Inside it were at least several hundred bots of various types, along with an equal number of spare parts kits and support tools for the different models. Each of the bots was wrapped in a tough, clear plastic container.

"How about that?" Jake said as we stood there bathing the bots in the light from our suits. "If we can get some of these back to our base . . ."

"*If*. That's not going to be easy given the limited space in the van," Nikki said.

"We can just use this cable," Jake patted the carbonylon cable he'd wrapped around his shoulder and under one arm, "String them up under the van."

"Sounds logical," I said, "only I'm afraid it won't work. The downward wash from the antigrav rods would cause anything below the van to either be knocked off or ripped apart. We'll have to fill the van then fasten them to the top and sides."

"We'd better fasten them carefully so the load won't shift around, too," Nikki said. "I can imagine what might happen if one swung loose and flopped around changing the balance of the van at a critical moment."

I thought about us hurtling toward the face of the Moon because of a poorly tied square knot.

"Are the bots operational?" Nikki asked.

"We'll see," Jake said. He stepped forward and pressed the release seam down the plastic cover. The cover opened; Jake reached in and flipped the control switch on. Nothing happened. "Looks like we may have some work to do. I wonder whether they lack batteries or just need to be charged. Anyone know how to open up a bot?"

"Just a minute," I said. "I had some bots like these over here in my lab." I bounced over to the bots. "Yeah, these are standard labbots in space man's clothing. Let me pop one open and check its energy pack." I pulled off the plastic container around it and tried the activation switch on the off chance that Jake had picked a malfunctioning bot. Like the other, the bot failed to come on.

I spent the next few seconds trying to remove the battery cover so that I could see inside the battery compartment. Suit lights are sure awkward; I had to do a contortionist act before I could see. "It has batteries but they aren't charged."

"How are we going to—"

"Shouldn't be too hard," I said. "We can run a cable off the van's generating system. It'll take a while but it'll work."

"I'll go get the van," Nikki said and bounded out of the room and down the dark hallway behind us.

"Let's move this one out to the door," I said. "It will be easiest to charge since I know how it operates. Unfortunately, the van's a little big to get down here where the bots are."

Jake came over and grabbed one side of the bot and I took the other. Through a series of spastic hops, we finally got it moved to the entrance of the storage area as Nikki brought the van nearby.

"You know," Nikki said, as she stepped out of the van, "we could program a couple of bots to drag the other bots to the entrance. It'd save a lot of work in the long run."

"Good idea," I said. I hated taking the time to program a bot, but the task was fairly simple and I hated carrying bots even more than programming them.

I pulled up the hood of the van and removed the coiled electrical cable that I had stored there. Setting the voltage regulator (which had come to us thanks to Jake's surplus gear) to the correct setting, I plugged one end of the cable into the bot's recharge panel and the other to the regulator. In five minutes, the bot was functional.

"Either of you know how to program one of these?" I asked.

"No."

" 'Fraid not."

So while Nikki and Jake played explorer, I got to play nursemaid to some very dim-witted machines. About a half hour later, the bot was finally dragging another bot out of the storage area and setting it by the van. I was relieved to see that it hadn't smashed the other bot in the process.

By transferring the program from the first bot to the second, I was able to have two bots bring out the others. I could have programmed several more, but found that with just the two working, I was able to charge a bot by the time they dragged out a new bot. I decided having a bot recharge the others was a little more risky than I wanted since the voltage regulator seemed to vary a lot and had to be constantly watched.

There were three models of bots. One was the cylindrical labbot that I was familiar with. The two other models looked like they'd probably both been designed for the low gravity of the moon since they had spidery legs. One was about the size of a small dog and had *Go-4* ("gopher," get it?) stenciled on the side of it, while the other had a body the size of a man's with eight-meter appendages that could be used as feet or hands, or could have power tools mounted on it. The crazy things could move on two appendages like a man or—if they had a heavy load—on four or more legs, which gave them a real bug look. In my mind at least, it looked like a spider.

After two hours of charging bots, I was finally finished. The bots stood beside the van waiting for more instructions. I had been listening to Jake and Nikki on the radio. They'd managed to get the computer running in the control room and pulled out a list of what was in the storage area. Now they were making sounds that you'd expect from two kids in a candy store. They'd found the manifest of what was in the storage area.

"I'm finished up out here if you two want to help load up," I said.

Moments later, Nikki bounced up to me, "Look at this." She handed me a computer printout.

I read some of the list. "Food, tools, medicine—looks like we could be set up for quite some time. My only question is, Will we be endangering some upcoming expedition if we use any of this?"

"Yeah, that's an angle we haven't really considered," Jake said. "I'd hate to move this out and cause some group to starve to death. I really think it's only an outside chance that anyone's planning on ever coming back, though. They've dismantled the space development and exploration."

"Even if a group came up from Earth," Nikki said, "if we can start up the mining operation, and make some rods, we'll be able to transport food and equipment up from Earth like there's no tomorrow. The need of a storage dump like this will be a thing of the past."

"Catering service. Hmmm. At any rate, we won't be needing these supplies for a long time," I said. "It'll be good to know that they're here if we should need them." I handed the list to Nikki. "It's hard to believe that they abandoned all this."

"That's the problem with chemical rockets. They're too expensive," Jake said. "It was cheaper to leave all this stuff here than take it back down. Just think of how things are going to change when the rods become available. A jump to the Moon will be as easy as a rocket flight to another part of the Earth."

"It's hard to imagine the effect the rods would have if we ever get enough made to make them available," I said.

"And once the public knows about them, we'll be out of danger," Nikki said.

"I don't know," I said. "If someone wanted to kill us before, they'll be interested in silencing us rather than letting the public find out that they tried to keep the rods under wraps."

14

Though the sun had hardly changed position, the Earth above us had rotated almost a half turn and our muscles were starting to complain even with the reduced gravity of the Moon. My stomach rumbled from time to time since I'd avoided trying to use the liquid garbage from the tubes designed for use with space suits.

The van was crammed full of bots. The little gophers filled in the spaces between the larger bots, and the spiders were stored endwise with all their legs folded. Added to this were the four cylindrical labbots fastened to each side of the van with four more tied to the top.

It'll never fly, I thought, though I knew better. Lifting off was not going to be a problem. Taking the full crew of humans was. And I knew that no one would take seriously my suggestion of strapping Jake to the hood of the van.

Finally we all got scrunched into our seats. Little gophers were fitted in all around each of us. I felt like a mother Saint Bernard.

"You know, this is pretty dangerous," I said. "One impact and they'll never sort the meat from the metal."

"Don't worry," Nikki said. "The computers will handle the whole thing."

So we lifted off on yet another terror express ride. Once I got the van up over the rim of the crater, the computer locked onto the beacon and we whisked off over the jagged mountain range at almost as great a speed as we'd traveled in with.

"You know, we could program a bot to fly this route and free us up to work at the base," Nikki said.

"I don't know—what if something broke down? There we'd be without a way to travel to repair it."

"Yeah, you're probably right. Once we get to manufacturing the rods, though, we'd be able to do something like that."

"We could even build a bot/computer vehicle that could be used just for such tasks."

"Like the rocket expresses back on Earth," Jake said from behind a pile of bots in the back.

"Don't remind me of the rockets on Earth," Nikki said, "I'm still bitter."

"Getting fired was the best thing that ever happened to you," I said. "Just think, you wouldn't be with us if you hadn't gotten canned. Instead of riding in a flying junkyard, you'd be sitting at home enjoying yourself."

"Not being in an itchy, sweat-filled suit wouldn't be without its finer points," Nikki said. "But I'm glad I'm here with— "

At that point, the computer failed and we dropped like a rock.

It was only a few moments before the second computer kicked in but I think we all thought we'd had it. Our downward drop was checked with what felt like a quick kick in the seat of the pants. Bots jostled and pushed against us and felt as if they were just this side of crushing us.

I quit screaming and calmly yelled, "What the hell happened!"

"Computer failed. Luckily the backup worked," Nikki said. She was fiddling with the first. "Program's gone."

"Jake, you OK?" I asked.

"Banged my nose, otherwise OK."

"I'm going to transfer the program back from computer two to one so we'll have a backup in case that happens again," Nikki said.

"Is that safe to do?" I asked. "What if—"

"Hold on," Nikki said.

I gritted my teeth.

"There," she said.

"That was kind of a letdown, no sparks, drops, or explosions," I said.

"Keep up the letdowns," Jake said.

"What caused the computer failure?" I asked.

"Probably a gamma ray. It doesn't happen often with the new memories but can—rarely—take place. Or the computer might have a more serious problem. I'm having it check itself out now . . . and . . . no problems. Must have been a stray gamma ray."

I eyed a sharp, jagged peak that we were just over. I could imagine my frail body impaled on it.

We reached our base without further mishap. We were all worn out so we called it a day and left the van to be unloaded the next day.

The next month was very eventful in that we got the bots organized and succeeded in getting both the mine and hydroponics dome operational. The three of us even managed to assemble the base's solar furnace without crisping any of us.

After Jake had created wire-drawing dies, we soon had bots making wire-and-armature-wrapping programs for the gophers. Shortly after that, we had several large generators ready and waiting to give us all the power we could possibly need—once we got the new rods manufactured to power the generators.

The tough part was making those first rods since we were short of power. We spent a lot of time during the long lunar nights using a minimum of power. Once we'd gotten those first rods made and mounted to the generators, though, things got pretty easy. Soon the bots were programmed to continue mining, smelting, and making rods.

Three months passed and about the most exciting thing that happened was that the synthaskin sloughed off Nikki's and my faces—causing a bit of wonderment for Jake, who hadn't seen just how beautiful Nikki really was. We had a huge stockpile of rods and were ready to return to Earth with the second step of our plan: to convince the Earth government to abandon old forms of power generation. It was going to be tricky since someone—maybe even everyone in power—was already out to keep my discovery a secret. But we figured that we would offer an ultimatum: integrate the rods into society or we would release the technology covertly in such a way as to topple the government.

Though things went well on a mechanical level during those three months, the same couldn't be said about things on a personal level. I think we were all anxious to get back to Earth. An automated plant isn't too exciting once it starts going, and the Moon, while it is pretty, doesn't have the color, warmth, or safety of Earth.

And I was depressed. Nikki was not unfriendly to me, just not overly friendly. Two men with one well-built woman in a small area just doesn't work very well. Another month and I suspect Jake and I would have been at each other's throats.

It was time to return to Earth.

15

It was a little disconcerting to leave what had become *our* Copernicus Base with only the bots in charge; more and more I was beginning to identify with the sorcerer's apprentice. I could imagine coming back to discover that the whole moon had been converted into gravity rods. But there was no other way; the bots had to be left to their own devices since a huge inventory of rods would be needed for projects we'd been planning for the near future. Nevertheless, it seemed that more and more my future seemed to hang in the balance of how well machines performed.

We took a few precautions to make sure that we weren't discovered: we disabled the homing beacon for our base and Jake painted some very realistic looking biological hazard signs, which he mounted all over the outside of the base's domes. It would take a very brave group of people to enter the base if an expedition should come up from Earth.

We had transported all of the rovers at the Eratosthenes Base by welding gravity rods to them. Each of the rovers had been converted with gravity rods so that they made their own power much as my van did. We converted one of the wheeled versions of the rovers further so that we could load it up with odds and ends and take it back to Earth with us. Strangely enough, the hard part wasn't getting the rover into flying form but rather getting it set up to travel on Earth roads once we got back to terra firma; since the rover had wheels, we hoped to tow it behind the van without raising too much interest. The rover was a lot of work but enabled us to carry back a number of the rods to Earth as well as the stuff we'd be needing for our next steps to get the antigrav technology released to Earth.

Our "Plan A" was a little simplistic and would require us to improvise a lot along the way. We hoped to confront whoever was trying to kill us off and bargain to release the secret of the rods in exchange for our secrecy about their trying to silence us. In the shuffle, we hoped to bargain for the possession of our Moon base (though we were going to keep it a secret unless we really thought things were going our way). Obviously, this would take some fast talking and maybe even the threat of releasing the secret of anti-gravity covertly, which would—with any luck at all—wreck the world economy in the process. And that was "Plan B": to release the secret of the rods covertly.

(While the secret of the antigravity technology could have made us rich, we figured that if we could continue with our automated mining-rod manufacturing operation on the Moon for a while, money wouldn't be a problem for us anyway.)

While Plan A was a little optimistic perhaps, it would be simpler to do than to try to release the technology as in Plan B. And Plan B could create a major social upheaval and would take forever and a day to carry out successfully without getting us all killed. But if Plan A failed, Plan B seemed our only alternative.

Either way, we knew it was going to be tough. You don't just walk up to someone who's trying to fill you full of holes and say, "Before you pull the trigger, I'd like to have a few words with your boss." At least you don't try that twice.

So we were going to have to find a way to talk to the "boss man" without getting killed in the process. And we didn't even know for sure who was out to get us. The world government? The energy cartel? Both? Neither?

We had our work cut out for us as we lifted off from the Moon.

"It's strange," Nikki said, "I'm going to be glad to get back to Earth. But I feel a little sad about leaving."

"Yeah," I said, "I feel that way, too. Guess it's nice

and safe here. Seeing the huge stack of antigravity rods the bots are churning up day in and day out is kind of exciting.''

''We're getting enough rods to carry out some fantastic work if we ever get the time and manpower to do it,'' Jake said. ''Before long, we're going to have to consider heading out to the asteroids. One chunk of an icy asteroid would take care of all our water needs for some time if we attached rods to it and hauled it back.''

''Spoken like a true spacer,'' I said with a chuckle.

''The possibilities really are endless,'' Nikki said.

''If we can get Earth off our backs,'' Jake said.

The rover floated behind our van. It worked in tandem to our controls. We'd rigged up a tow bar between the vehicles that carried messages from our van's computer to another computer we'd looted from the Eratosthenes Base and mounted in the rover. This would enable it to follow our maneuvers—we hoped. If it came loose or the packaging came apart, there were enough rods aboard to take off to the next galaxy. We were towing a lot of potential mayhem and destruction. I tried to think about other things.

We raced around the Moon twice and then started the jump through space. Many hours later, the beautiful blue and white of Earth swelled below our feet. We waited for the scheduled rocket flight that would be dropping into Houston. Our good luck continued as it was close enough to schedule for us to match its downward arc. After a few teeth-wrenching changes of velocity, we were back off Galveston Island, hugging the waves as we skimmed toward land. By driving all night, we reached Jake's surplus shop as the sun was rising. The worst thing that happened to us was that our vehicles picked up a few bullet holes when we had to drive through some feuding motorists.

Jake's shop was intact and his nephew, Mark, in one piece. That was a relief. While Jake and Nikki hadn't apparently been worried about anything happening to Mark, after the way the big lady had found me, I had started to feel like we were facing supernatural foes.

Mark had done a good job. He'd sold off all of Nikki's jewelry and the industrial laser and gotten some good prices for them. Even so, it hadn't been quite enough to get him by so he'd also sold Jake's antique sports car rather than any of the space gear. Though Jake had specifically ordered him not to sell any of the surplus gear (since we might be wanting it), I could see that Jake didn't aim to have his car get less than priority treatment. I thought maybe Jake would turn Mark into a human pretzel; to my disappointment, there was no such show.

After living in the low gravity of the Moon for three months, just sitting on Earth was work. Even getting my eyelids back up when blinking took an effort. While we'd exercised in the tiny gym at our base, it didn't take up all the slack for muscles gone soft. We felt like birds with their wings clipped; where before we'd been able to nearly fly over the landscape, now we walked with plodding steps or—in Jake's case—dragged about on crutches.

In addition to physical problems, our mental problem was nearly as overwhelming as the heavy gravity. We had to figure out how to contact whoever was in charge of rubbing us out. Of course we could have ignored them and laid low. That had worked for the last three months. But if those who were concerned about the rods found that we were actually manufacturing them again, the search for us would probably be larger and less subtle than before. I didn't care to spend every day of my existence wondering if the trash bots were about to cram me into the garbage truck or if the mail bot was really a hit man in disguise. Life in such a condition would slowly drive me mad—without the "slowly."

And if they did locate us . . . imagining a screaming fighter plane dropping a few barrels of napalm onto Jake's happy store didn't do much for me either. I had no desire to become a crispy critter.

"So how can we get to them before they get to us?" Nikki asked as we sat around the table munching on a small salad that Mark had prepared for us—apparently with an ax judging from the state of the vegetables in it.

"Perhaps we can turn the tables on them," I said. "It'd be hard, but if we planned it carefully, maybe we could trap whoever comes to get us."

"That might work but it sounds pretty dangerous," Nikki said.

"Yes, it will be that. The last person they sent after us was pretty effective," I shuddered a bit as I thought about the headless bag lady. The Russian salad dressing looked nauseatingly like blood; I decided to use the creamy. "But we have some tricks up our sleeves this time. While they think we're on our own and probably all but out of money, we actually have Jake and quite a few resources, thanks to the gear we brought back from the Moon."

"Why don't we get a decoy van set up?" Jake said. "We could buy another old shell like your van and—"

"Put the old numbers on it. . . . We could even convert it to antigrav travel," Nikki said.

"Yeah," I said, and munched for a moment on a piece of celery. "If we had two vans instead of one, that would really throw them off." The possibilities were looking like they could be shifted a bit more in our favor.

"Well, anyway, if we can get someone to come after us . . ." So one salad and several hours later, our plan had been pretty well formed.

Our first step in this plan was to get a decoy van set up. We had too much equipment wired into the original van to sacrifice it, so we decided to barter for an old van to use as the decoy. After trading off an industrial laser we'd brought back in the rover, we were able to obtain a van to convert to a nearly identical copy of our old van. After that, Jake—who had a lot of skill at doing body work on cars—cut off the storage area he'd added to the top of our old van and filled in the bullet holes it had picked up on the road. Then we repainted them both so that the new van looked like the old one while my old, original one looked completely different.

In order not to bring attention to Jake's business, we decided to make contact with our enemies far away from Galveston. Since New Denver had been the last place we'd been seen by them (we hoped), that seemed like a logical place to begin. We loaded up the two vans with special goodies and we followed a rocket from Houston back into New Denver (this time we mimicked its whole ballistic arc by wearing space suits for the short trip).

Nikki rode with me, which really made my day. Jake

looked pretty disappointed but I didn't feel bad enough to suggest that Nikki ride with him.

From the New Denver rocket port, we headed back to Kraig's condo, since that seemed like the most likely spot to strike pay dirt in our search for our enemies.

I knew it was risky since it was entirely possible that the apartment had been booby-trapped. We gambled on the fact that the people we were facing seemed to be interested in doing things so that they appeared to be accidental or so that the person would vanish without a trace. That took the personal touch of someone like the bag-lady pro we'd faced last time I'd been in the apartment. Also, since I'd been free so long, we figured that they would be concerned about interrogating me to be sure there weren't other new loose ends they needed to cut off.

Nikki and I left the decoy van on the street where I'd parked before and went up to her place. Jake—who was our ace in the hole—waited on the street in my original van.

After taking the elevator up, we stood in the doorway of her condo a moment; then I gritted my teeth and had Nikki use her thumbprint to dilate the door. I had known that something was wrong when the elevator had worked with Nikki's thumbprint. Now I was sure. Kraig would have changed the lock after tossing Nikki out. I tossed in my suitcase and stepped back. Nothing exploded so I stepped in and waited a moment, half expecting something or someone to cut me to ribbons. Nothing happened; it seemed to be safe.

Nikki stepped in behind me and closed the door. We walked through the living room into the hall and entered the kitchen. We put the bags down on the kitchen counter and quickly ran through the apartment.

"Nice to see that someone cleaned up the decapitated bag lady we left behind," Nikki said.

"Certainly is. Looks like everything else is as we left it. Now all we need to—"

Jake's voice crackled over the ear radio I was wearing. "Got a bag lady nosing around your van."

"Rats," I said into my throat microphone. "I'd hoped for a bit more time. OK, we'll rush around up here."

Nikki and I hurried with our jobs. I popped open the suitcase I'd brought in and removed the industrial spray coater we'd brought back from the Moon. I started spraying a plastic cover over all the air vents in the apartment then shut off the climate computer so that it wouldn't burn itself out trying to adjust the temperature in the rooms. That done, I sealed off the doors to the other rooms except for the kitchen and the hallway connecting the living room and kitchen area. There was no sign of Kraig or anyone else.

Nikki pushed the couch and chair back into the floor so that the living room was all carpet, then started getting the suitcases in the kitchen ready for our upcoming confrontation.

Jake's voice came on again, "The bag lady's either talking to herself or over a microphone. I'm still not sure this is one of the ones we're wanting."

"OK," I said. "Let us know if she heads for the building."

"Sorry but she's headed your way now," Jake said. "She took something out of her bag as she entered the front. Good luck you two. Holler if you need help."

We'll be needing the luck for sure, I thought, as I made a hole from the living-room wall into the kitchen with a screwdriver. I hoped we wouldn't be needing more help than Jake could give us. This bag lady hadn't given us enough time to get everything done we'd hoped to.

I inspected the tiny peephole I'd made as Nikki got the 3V going. I turned to see a complex pattern of pulsating green circles that slowly turned blue as they rose out of the floor. The circles grew into spheres and blinked from one color to another. They grew into overlapping patterns filling every bit of space in a three-dimensional polka-dot pattern that continued to flash to different hues with the gonging music that throbbed with them. Up and down no longer seemed to be in the right places as the spheres started circling the room rapidly, then tilted off on a plane all their own.

"Good grief, Nikki, does anyone enjoy watching that kind of stuff? It makes me feel sick."

"That's my favorite 3V disk! You can apologize later." She leaned over and turned off the sound, then took me by the hand to keep me from walking in circles. I closed my eyes to the dizzying sight and let her lead me.

She got me into the kitchen just as the front door gave us a warning beep and dilated open. I peeked through the hole in the wall. A bag lady, identical to the one we'd fought before, stepped in. The thing Jake had seen her pull out of her bag was a bullpup combat shotgun.

18

She shut the door behind her as transparent pink bubbles chased by blue cubes swirled around her. Nikki and I put on oxygen masks.

She tried to see through the clutter produced by the 3V machine. The safety on her shotgun clicked audibly in the quiet apartment; she proceeded to fire twenty quick shots all around her. I ducked down behind the counter in the kitchen, hoping the cabinet would absorb the impact of the shot. I was thankful we'd hidden in the kitchen rather than trying to remain concealed in the 3V patterns.

I'd lost track of how many shots she'd fired at seventeen but—over the ringing in my ears—heard the empty magazine of her shotgun pop out of her weapon and knew that it was the "now or never" time.

I picked up one of the bottles from the suitcase Nikki had opened up. Walking like a duck along the kitchen floor to the doorway, I tossed the bottle into the living room.

The plan was that the bottle would break. It didn't.

Instead the heavy glass bounced on the thick carpeting and the bag lady got a good idea of exactly where we were. She slapped a fresh magazine into the shotgun.

"Take the lid off the bottles first," Nikki whispered and threw her bottle around the corner.

I followed her example and we both quickly chugged another pair of the glass bottles around the corner as shotgun blasts riddled the doorjamb. Some of the liquid spilled into the kitchen as we threw the bottles. The fumes were nearly overpowering even with our oxygen masks on. Nikki and I each held our breaths. Things were getting quiet in the next room but we opened four more bottles and threw them around the corner into the living room just to be safe.

It was still quiet in there.

Had our plan worked? we wondered. We waited a few more minutes.

All remained quiet.

And my kidneys made me feel like the bathroom was more of a concern than the living room. Fear does not bring out the hero in my body, I decided, as I got up the nerve to peek into the living room through the peephole.

The bag lady was crumpled on the carpet, looking like a pile of rags. Above her danced a group of red cubes that were slowly descending, looking as if they'd crush her.

"The old bat probably never quite realized what had happened; she just kept breathing until she passed out from the fumes. I hope," I told Nikki as well as Jake over the throat mike. "I'll check her out. Cross your fingers and come on up, Jake."

With my Beretta trained on her, I carefully walked up to her body (which wasn't easy with red and purple squares dancing through the room). I kicked the shotgun away from her then reached down and removed the flesh-colored ballistic mask from her face. Her eyes were closed and the sound of a snore greeted my ears.

Nikki turned off the 3V then brought out the plastic wrap machine and I covered the bag lady's body in a sheet of plastic so that only her head remained free. Once we were sure she wasn't going anywhere, we opened up the vents in the room to let air into it. After things had aired out, we removed our masks and let Jake in.

We tried to plan on what to do next. We knew that the assassin wouldn't be an easy person to break.

Fortunately, she helped us out.

"Look at this," Nikki said after she had dumped the contents of the bag lady's handbag onto the carpet. In addition to six magazines of spare ammunition, a small talkie, and two hand grenades, there was also a small medical kit of some type. Nikki carefully opened it. It contained a number of vials and two old-style hypodermic needles.

"What do you suppose that's for?" I asked.

Jake laughed. "I think I know. Let me take a look." Nikki handed the pouch to him and he took out one of the vials and examined it. "Yep. Though they're not normally packaged with that type of hypodermic needle—I'm sure these are vials of truth serum."

"What?" Nikki and I said in unison.

"Yeah, they used to test us out with that stuff before they'd let us go into space. Tried to be sure we wouldn't steal them blind. Can't figure why she'd have that, though."

"Maybe this is the reason," I said, holding up one of the rounds of spare ammunition she had in her bag. "These aren't ordinary loads she was shooting at us. Look at the marks on the walls. They hardly made a dent."

Jake pried one of the spent projectiles out of the wall. "Looks like a liquid-filled load. Poison?"

"No, I'll bet they're stun shells," I said.

"Maybe she was going to disable us and then . . ." Nikki started and stopped in midsentence.

"Then quiz us," I said. "That way she could find out if someone else knew about the rods. Makes sense."

"There's one way to find out," Jake said, holding the truth serum kit.

"Can you get her to babble away?" I asked. "How will you know what dosage?"

"This stuff is pretty safe to use. You'd need a high dose to hurt someone. Least that's what they used to tell us. Besides, she wasn't exactly out to give you a good time. Let's give her the drug before she has a chance to come to. That way she'll be less apt to resist if she's been programmed to resist truth serum."

"If you think you know what you're doing," I said.

After we gave her a shot and a few whiffs from an oxygen mask, she was ready to talk. Our questions were very straightforward:

"Who do you work for?"

"I-don't-know."

"How did they communicate with you?"

"Over-my-talkie."

"After catching the people in the condo, how will you tell your boss you've succeeded?"

"Over-my-talkie."

"What will you tell him?"

"Mission-successful. Will-bring-in."

"Write that down, Nikki, the order of the words might be part of a code or something so they know it's really the bag lady. Do you know where to find some paper here?" I said.

Nikki scrambled into the kitchen and returned with a pad, "Ask her again so we get it right."

We did and Nikki quickly wrote it down and continued to take notes as we questioned the bag lady.

"Bring them in to where?"

"Will-get-coordinates-with-call."

"Why did she have the truth serum if she was to just bring us in?" Nikki asked.

The bag lady answered the question before we could put it to her. "Was-to-question-all-of-them. Ask-about-others-connected-to-group-and-eliminate-all-but-one-who-knows-of-others."

We continued to question the bag lady until we'd gotten passwords, methods of doing things, and so forth. We tried to get everything from her that might be of help.

As we were finishing up with our questions, her eyes fluttered a bit and her face turned bright red. "She's coming around," Jake said. "We could safely give her another dose."

"I don't have any more questions," I said. "Do either of you?"

They both shook their heads no.

"Then why don't we—"

"What's she doing?" Nikki asked.

Good question. The woman moved her mouth and made a horrible face. Too late I realized what was happening. "I bet she just poisoned herself," I said. I tried to pull her mouth open but she held it locked shut and made an evil-looking face at me until I quit trying. Moments later as we helplessly watched, the woman gave a shudder, exhaled a long breath, and was dead.

Her jaw relaxed and I pulled it open and I saw the

hollow tooth that was loose on her tongue. "An old but effective trick." I felt for the pulse in her neck. Dead.

We all realized that the people we were up against were completely ruthless. It was time for the next step of our plan. Out of the frying pan and into the fire, I thought.

17

After a ghoulish exercise in undressing the dead body, Nikki was dressed in the bag lady's ballistic armor and clothes. That done, I showed Nikki how to operate the combat shotgun. We loaded it with the stun shells since we hoped to take a prisoner or two at our next stop.

While we all crossed our fingers, Nikki called over the bag lady's talkie. We received instructions to leave the van on the street and bring in the prisoner—me—and information to receive the bag lady's—Nikki's—pay. We had a tense moment when the man on the other end of things asked what vehicle we'd be arriving in.

What had the bag lady been driving and would whoever we were meeting know what she should be driving?

Or was it a trick?

"I'll be driving my new blue van," Nikki said into the talkie then closed her eyes tightly as if expecting to be hit.

A pause while Jake and I held our breaths.

"OK," came the voice over the talkie. "Here's how you get to us . . ."

Before we left, we booby-trapped our decoy van. Anyone who tried to operate it without the proper computer code would discover himself flying at maximum speed—straight up. Though it would mean sacrificing one of our vans, it would probably be worth it, I figured, since that would get at least one undesirable off the face of the Earth.

Nikki drove and I sat in the passenger's seat. Jake sat in his office chair. We had an improvised curtain—borrowed from Kraig's condo—that hid Jake from casual inspection.

We all wore our throat mikes and earphones so we could communicate with Jake, who'd be left behind in the van when we got to our destination.

Our meeting was to take place in the Catacombs. If Jake and I had known about the Catacombs before we got into the van with Nikki, we would not have gotten into the van with Nikki.

"Where are the Catacombs?" I asked. I had in mind some resort area in the mountains. Maybe some caves or something.

After Nikki filled us in, I came in with a little different idea. It was simple really: If you take the beauty of the Col-Kan sky and the jeweled, needle skyscrapers of New Denver and then imagine just the opposite of all that, you have a pretty good idea of what the Catacombs are.

The Catacombs were originally huge parking areas for those living and working in the buildings of New Denver. They were interconnected so that the residents could move around the small city, visit, or go shopping even during a heavy snow storm. But like a lot of other major projects, the system was poorly thought out. Even when everything was new, the parking lots had seldom been used since most of those who lived in the buildings weren't home much; the condos were owned by those who would be traveling worldwide via the rocket port. Such people seldom fooled with owning a vehicle of their own. When they needed to travel in New Denver, they took taxi-bots or even choppers to get around.

So the underground network had been crime-ridden from the beginning. As the system was used less and less, maintenance was discontinued. Finally, decades after they were built, the underground areas had turned into a veritable no-man's-land where criminals, Night Creeps, and other lowlifes roamed unchecked.

"And," Nikki told us as we ignored the warning signs and turned down the short street leading to one of the few unsealed Catacombs entrances, "rumor has it that the Catacombs have even been expanded to accommodate those living in them."

"Rumor? Doesn't anyone know?" Jake asked.

"Those who found out whether the rumors were true or

not never lived long enough to tell about it,'' Nikki answered.

''Don't ever tell me any bedtime stories,'' I said.

''Don't worry.''

Ugh, I thought. Shot down in flames.

Nikki turned on the van's headlights as we left the sunlit street and started down the dark ramp leading into the Catacombs. It suddenly felt colder in the van.

''Jake, have your needle rifle ready. Looks like we could be needing it on the way in,'' I said.

''Already have it out,'' Jake said.

I picked up the Colt assault rifle I'd taken from the pukers and draped it across my lap. If Nikki had been trying to scare us, she'd succeeded.

The headlights of our van illuminated various dust-covered junked vehicles with most of their windows broken in, leaving jagged teeth in all their openings. Empty cans and trash littered the area as far as the headlights poked light into the darkness before us. We passed through a screen of dense, black smoke, which seeped into the van; someone was burning rubber tires. Fortunately we soon escaped from the thick swirling screen and broke into relatively clear—if dusty—air.

As we journeyed down the cavelike corridor of gray concrete, more and more rusted-out vehicles littered either side of the narrow ramp. Nikki made a turn and we passed a large area where great chunks of concrete had been blasted from the walls and lay along the road. Another turn led us out of the rubble and down an undamaged section.

Now we occasionally saw vehicles with their windows intact; the glass was painted or stained so that whatever was inside them was obscured.

''There're lights inside some of those cars,'' Nikki said.

''Do you suppose people live in them?'' Jake asked peeking through the curtain.

''Maybe.'' I wondered what kind of person would give up the light of day to live in the trash and darkness.

''We turn left here,'' Nikki said. We slowed and started down another passageway that looked identical to the others. Nikki had memorized the route as it had been given to her. I was totally lost already.

We went nearly a mile without turning and then made several more quick turns and journeyed downward on a narrow, dirty ramp. Human shapes often danced in the shadows on either side of us as we passed. Other nonhuman forms jumped away from the beam of our headlights while large rodents darted across our path from time to time with their red eyes gleaming.

Farther from the entrance of the Catacombs, cars and other obstacles became rarer. Nikki speeded up.

We made another turn and again the headlights revealed a mosaic of trash and junk along our path. Papers and old newsfax blew in the van's wake as we hurtled past. Piles of rags that looked terrifyingly like bodies appeared alongside the road; these piles of rags were interspersed with the glistening white bones of large animals—or men—that had been picked clean by the rats that scurried out of sight as we passed. We occasionally heard the sound of bones crunching under our wheels.

After seeing no cars for some time, we rounded a curve to see, in the gloom ahead of us, a group of crouching, stripped vehicles. As we hurtled toward them, an old truck slowly rolled from its parking berth beside the bodies of the cars around it. The truck picked up speed as we neared it.

"Hang on, Jake, looks like someone's trying to block our path," I said.

I clicked the safety off my rifle, opened the vent window, and jammed the barrel out it.

"Hang on to your ears," I said and let loose a three-round burst of bullets at the truck. My ears ached at the sound. The truck continued to roll as we came upon it.

I fired another burst as Nikki floored the accelerator and, with a screech of tires, we skidded around it. A group of men or women—it was impossible to tell which with the dirt and the rags they wore—sprang in front of us. They threw rocks at the van.

"Don't slow down," I told Nikki.

All but one got out of the way. The van made a sickening lurch as it crushed our would-be assailant.

"Oh, no," Nikki cried.

"You can't help that," Jake said. "They're trying to kill us. Don't worry about hurting them."

A crash and the sound of metal being strained came from behind us. Something large had hit the back of the van. Jake's curses echoed through the van.

"Everything OK back there?" I asked.

"Yeah. We're going to have some more bodywork to do when we get back though."

"Just so our hides remain intact," I said, pulling my rifle back into the van and closing the vent window. I thumbed the rifle's selector back to safe position.

We flew through the darkness. The area was again free of vehicles and Nikki was taking advantage of the fact to speed ahead.

"This area looks clear. There isn't so much junk," Nikki said.

"Not only that," I said. "Look at the walls. Plastic. We've left the original Catacombs area. This must have been added to the underground network fairly recently."

"Who would want to add to this mess?"

A bright light shone ahead of us. Its beam seemed to cut a tunnel in the dust that hung in the air and glistened off the blue plastic walls.

"We turn here, I think," Nikki said as we approached a fork in the plastic tubing. I hoped she wasn't lost. Spending days to find our way out didn't exactly sound like a fun-filled way to pass the time.

As we rounded the smooth plastic corner, the walls expanded into a huge chamber. The area was bathed in a purple light. A bag lady—identical to the other two who'd attacked us—stood inside a sandbag bunker directly in front of us. She trained an ancient M60 machine gun on us.

I swore under my breath, "Careful. That thing could riddle our van." I hoped the bag lady was in a better mood than those of her sisters we'd encountered in the recent past. They all looked exactly alike. I realized that the bag ladies actually wore some sort of a uniform with identical patches and bulletproof face masks. Identical down to the tilt of the battered cloth hat.

Nikki slowed almost to a stop.

I held my breath.

The bag lady looked into the van then motioned us on

when she saw that Nikki—in bag lady's clothing—was driving.

We drove across the chamber and entered another long plastic tube.

A string of small blue lights dotted the walls and pointed our way to us. Ten minutes later, the tube expanded and the lights became brighter and brighter as we drove on. After perhaps a mile we entered a large cavern, so huge that it was impossible to see the far side of it. The field ahead of us was circled by yellow floodlights.

"Can you believe this?" Nikki said as she slowed the van to a stop.

I couldn't.

A two-story, white Colonial-style house stood in front of us. Large trees and shrubs had been carefully planted around it and a well-manicured lawn covered the floor of the chamber. A small bird flew by the van and a deer bounded across the lawn as we watched.

"Well, I'll be a . . ." Jake said as he peeked through the curtains in the back of the van.

As I looked at the scenic area ahead of us, I decided we were dealing with someone who had taken an overdose of weird.

18

Nikki picked up the shotgun. I put down the assault rifle and wrapped myself in the remains of the clear plastic shell we'd used to wrap up the bag lady in Kraig's apartment. We'd cut it off her after she'd died. Now I draped it around myself hoping to make whoever was in the house think that I was bound.

"OK, Nikki. Tape me in," I said.

She reached over and fastened it with some short strips of tape.

Though it looked like I had been gift wrapped in industrial plastic, I could, I hoped, push my arms out and free myself since only the small plastic strips of tape held the shell in place. My trusty Beretta was stuck in my pants under my shirttails.

"Ready?" I asked Nikki and Jake.

"As ready as I'm going to get," Nikki said. She jumped out of the van and walked around and opened my door. She waited for me to get out.

"Nikki, you're going to have to act more menacing than that. Remember that you're a tough old bat," I said.

With that bit of prompting, she pulled me out and I gracefully fell on my side. I stood up and the plastic shell fell off me.

I swore under my breath and picked it up quickly. "Let's hope no one is watching," I said. "Can you fasten that back on?"

"Yeah. I hope the sticky isn't too full of dirt—I think that'll hold."

"OK. Remember the plastic is just taped on, but keep up the tough-gal act."

I immediately regretted telling her that since she gave me a sharp poke with the shotgun so I'd start toward the house. "I hope the safety on that blunderbuss is engaged," I said. "I'd hate to have to get a dose of stun shell."

"Shut up, pig," Nikki said.

"I've created a Frankenstein," I whispered to myself, forgetting about the throat mike. Jake's laughter sounded in my earphone.

We walked across the thick grass and stepped onto the porch. The white wooden door opened on its own.

I hesitated at the door. "Get on in there," Nikki growled loudly. I hoped someone was in there to hear her. It impressed me; I jumped right in.

I stumbled into the darkness of the room. My eyes quickly adjusted and I saw yet another bag lady sitting behind an antique oak desk in front of me.

"I've brought the prisoner," Nikki said.

The bag lady behind the desk pushed a button and a large panel of the wall opened up to reveal a dark passageway. "Take him on in."

With a shove from behind to remind me who was boss, I stepped forward and moved down the red brick hallway, which had apparently been designed by Edgar Allan Poe. The heavy wooden door at the end of it swung open as we reached it.

We found ourselves in a room with three-meter-high ceilings and Early American furniture. The tables in the room were cluttered with knickknacks, and cheap-looking pictures hung on the walls. The carpeting had a blue checkered pattern while the walls had red-and-white stripes. A fireplace between the windows crackled cheerily with a fake-looking electric flame. The room was a monument to poor taste.

"Well," a huge black man, dressed like Abe Lincoln, got up from one of the chairs as we entered. "Finally, we meet," he said in a syrupy bass voice. His eyes twinkled with an evil gleam. "Won't you have a seat, Mr. Hunter." He motioned to one of the stuffed chairs.

Turning toward Nikki, he said, "I'd like for you to stay

a moment to, uh, tidy up the loose ends to our business when Mr. Hunter and I are finished talking.''

I sat down. He eased his tall frame into a chair and gave me a mirthless grin that exposed a row of sharp white teeth. He smoothed the sleeve of his black jacket for a moment before speaking.

''We lost a good man when we tried to bring in your van. That doesn't make me very happy.''

''Good men are hard to find, no doubt.''

''I'd heard you had a smart mouth, Mr. Hunter.''

''Phil, please. We should be on a first-name basis.''

''You can call me Ejil Lincoln,'' he said. He flashed another of his heart-freezing smiles. ''Perhaps we should loosen your tongue and waste less time. Let's use the truth drugs,'' he said, again looking at Nikki.

''OK, Nikki, it looks like he's not going to tell us anything without help,'' I said.

Ejil Lincoln seemed to realize that something was not right. He sprang toward a small two-barreled flintlock pistol that was concealed among the clutter of the table next to him.

Nikki followed the motion with her shotgun and fired two quick shots as he grasped the pistol.

I knew stun shells don't work instantly. It took a couple of seconds for the drug to be carried through the bloodstream to the brain. So I didn't just sit in the chair to see what happened. I jumped toward Lincoln as he reached for the pistol.

Nikki's first shot nearly hit me.

The second hit Lincoln in the neck. He held the stock of the pistol and I grasped the barrel. He wrenched it from my fingers and shoved me away. He ignored Nikki and aimed the pistol at me. Nikki fired another shot, which struck his hand as he pulled the trigger. He fired—but the shot went wide.

He aimed again.

And fell right on top of me. It felt as if a giant redwood had toppled over.

''What's going on in there?'' Jake hollered in my earphone after hearing my groan.

''Phil's goofing off again,'' Nikki laughed nervously.

"Don't listen to her," I said after I'd finally regained my breath.

"Is everything OK?" Jake sounded a little exasperated.

"Yeah. How's it out there?" I asked as I pushed Ejil Lincoln—or whoever he was—off me.

"Looks clear."

"Good. We're going to quiz Mr. Nice in here and see if we can get a ticket to the next stop. This may be it, but I doubt it. I suspect he's just another hired hand," I said.

One needle prick and vial of serum later, Ejil Lincoln's tongue became quite loose.

We discovered that he was working for World Energy. That made sense; they stood to suffer the most if the antigrav technology become generally used; at the same time it was all but crazy since the rods could be harnessed into large generators as easily as small. Knowing how the average guy on the street hates to fuss around with mechanical things, I could imagine that most people would continue to buy power regardless of how it was generated. Only now, the power rates could actually be reduced.

That was academic at this point, though. Our first task was to get to the chairman of the board, Sammy Dobrynin. The man who ran and all but owned World Energy, thanks to a Russian ancestor who'd been a general and had the good fortune to have become a capitalist just as the Soviet empire had collapsed. By quickly taking over the Near East oil fields, which the Soviets had stolen from the Arabs, he had created an instant empire that had been jealously guarded by General Gorshov Dobrynin's heirs.

We fed Lincoln questions:

"Do you ever see Mr. Dobrynin?"

"Yes. When-I-have-important-business."

"Would you see him after the Hunter interview?"

"Yes."

"Were you to meet today?"

"Yes."

And so forth. Little by little we pulled the information from him. We also extracted his hollow toothful of poison and cleaned out his mouth so he couldn't pull a disappearing act.

In the end we had one Ejil Lincoln, the information

about where and how he'd be meeting Dobrynin, and no good way to get into the Dobrynin quarters, which were in the middle of Miami.

"Any ideas, Jake?" I asked into my throat mike.

"Well . . . not really. We can follow the shuttle that Ejil was to have taken. That would get us to Miami. But from there, you've got me."

We were all quiet for a moment while we thought.

"Hey, Phil," Jake said.

"Yeah."

"Look in that truth serum kit. Seems to me I saw an auto-suggest vial. I don't know much about that but I think maybe we could get Lincoln to do a little work for us."

"What does auto-suggest do?"

"You can feed them ideas to act on. You plant the idea and then let him think he's in charge. That kind of thing."

"So Lincoln could take Phil and me with him to Dobrynin?" Nikki said. "We could even make up some sort of excuse to get you in, Jake."

"Might work. Funny, Lincoln doesn't look like a Trojan horse," I said.

Nikki had the kit open and we read the different vials.

"Are there any instructions?" I asked her. Then I noticed the small speaker on the case. "Just a minute. It looks like it has a built-in guide. There. Try that button."

Nikki pressed it.

"Can I help you?" the case asked in a tiny mechanical voice.

"Yeah. We were wondering how the auto-suggestion hypno serum works."

The little kit told us all we needed to know. Shortly we had Ejil Lincoln all primed to do an act for us.

Lincoln, Nikki, and I went back to the van after a quick call to set things up with the head man. Then we raced out of the Catacombs.

We had a rocket to catch.

19

Apparently, the staff of the rocket port was used to having Ejil Lincoln and his bag ladies carry arms through the checkpoints. A uniformed security guard didn't even blink while Nikki, Lincoln, and I walked through the detectors and set off alarm bells in our wake. The guard shifted his weight from one foot to the other and gave a salute in the form of a yawn as we passed.

Lincoln put his Mastivisa into a machine and paid for the three of us. The machine told us thank-you and we walked up the plastic ramp into the crew compartment of the rocket. We crouched as we stepped from the loading ramp into the narrow confines of the first class section.

With some trepidation, we'd decided to leave Jake behind in New Denver. Since the rocket was taking off in the middle of the day, there was no good way for the van to follow it and we hated to leave it behind. Also, it would be pretty hard to get Nikki and me into Sammy Dobrynin's hideaway, let alone a third member.

So our plan was for Jake to follow the first rocket for Miami after darkness fell and, if all went well, to pick us up in Miami that night. The way Jake flew, I privately felt we'd be lucky if he landed somewhere within two hundred kilometers of Miami; we'd probably have to swim to get to the van. Making things doubly hard was the fact that none of us had ever been in Miami. Therefore, to simplify things, we decided to just meet at the rocket port parking area there.

After flying in the van, rocket flight seemed crude. We

were strapped into heavily padded seats inside a cabin that
was the size of a large drainpipe and that had the same
cheery interior that one would expect from a drainpipe.
The first leg of the journey we spent scrunched back into
the seats with our belly buttons leaning against our spines.
Then we fell weightlessly for enough time to make break-
fast stumble halfway into our throats, and finally enjoyed
some high-G slowing down that threatened to turn our
tortured navels wrongside out. At the end of our flight, we
floated into the Miami port without power—rockets are
just fancy gliders when they land and there's just one
chance to get down. And the lack of power makes it
impossible to try again if they mess up on the first pass.

As the ship shivered toward the landing strip, I closed
my eyes and tried not to think about the fact that all that
was in the captain's place was a bot or maybe just a hunk
of metal and plastic screwed into the wall somewhere.

With a bounce that I felt for sure spelled the end, we
skidded to a stop. A bot built like a stewardess with a
smile painted permanently to its face helped me get to
my shaky feet. The bot had what might have been mis-
taken for a dress into which she'd been poured—and forgotten to say when. She/it guided me to the disembarking
ramp.

Since the gradual warm-up of the atmosphere over the
first half of the twenty-first century had melted a lot of
the polar caps, Miami was another of the many cities along the
coast that was ringed by protective dikes.

The rocket port was an octopuslike affair to the north of
the walled city, with landing strips extending out from its
hub. We made our way to the tram, which took us over the
ocean into the city.

As we hung over the ocean, I inspected the city. It
looked like a sunken little island in the middle of the
ocean. Miami was a strange hodgepodge of ancient high-
rise buildings made of concrete and glass, new needle
buildings, and—as I discovered when we stepped off the
tram car into the parking lot of the rocket port—wall-to-
wall humanity. When you walked anywhere in Miami, you
had to be careful not to step on those sleeping—or
recovering—on the plastic or concrete walkways. Door-

ways were beds; real beds were occupied in shifts; whole families lived on stairways. When the poor lost their homes underwater, they hadn't left Miami, they'd just changed their addresses. Now, each person in the city had a square meter of space all his own at any given moment.

"Here it is," Lincoln said, as a large pink limousine pulled to the curb, nearly running over a puker who was lying there. The car was embellished in chrome; it was a car that would have seemed gaudy to a pimp.

I held the door so Lincoln could climb in. Although he was acting according to our programming, he still thought he was in control and neither Nikki nor I risked crossing him for fear we might undo his performance. We weren't sure just how far the drugs could be trusted to make him do what we wanted.

"Take us to Dobrynin," Lincoln said over the intercom.

"The villa?"

"Is Dobrynin there?"

"He will be after the game."

"No. Take us to wherever he is right now," Lincoln said. "We have important information and can't afford to wait in his villa."

The driver pulled away and threw us all back into the plush pink snakeskin upholstery of the car. Lincoln opened up the small bar in front of us and poured himself a drink. "You two want anything? I always take advantage of Dobrynin's free goodies," he confided to me with a wink as he stuffed four cigars into the breast pocket of his suit; a small vial of some type of drugs followed the cigars into their hiding place.

I was thirsty. "I'd like a Pepsicoke."

"Nothing, thanks," Nikki said.

I nearly spilled the drink when our limo rammed a small modif-horse and rider. I had noticed the plowlike attachment on the car's bumper; now I knew what it was for. Lincoln didn't blink. Apparently this was the practice followed by all polite drivers in Miami.

Most of those in front of us got out of our way. As we neared the stadium that had been carved out of the center of the city, we hit more and more pedestrians with stomach-wrenching regularity. While most of them were pukers or druggies, it still made me ill. Nikki scrunched down into her seat and tried not to look.

The limo pulled around the side entrance of the stadium, avoiding the long line of people waiting to purchase tickets. The stadium was made of pink and purple plastic and extended eighteen stories into the air.

Lincoln gave me his evil grin. "There's your energy dollars at work. Biggest stadium in the world."

I could believe it. "Also the most hideous."

As we stepped from the car, a group of bag ladies formed up around us; I lost Nikki among the look-alikes. Sweat popped out all over me and it wasn't because of the hot, humid climate. This is it, I thought, time for the showdown.

We stepped into a large elevator. There was only room for two bag ladies. Had Nikki made it in? There was no way of telling since all of those who'd met us carried shotguns. I wondered if it would be possible to head back down the elevator and just send our message from some safe place—like Antarctica.

We reached the top and headed down a long, pink hallway. Pink had never been my favorite color; it was quickly falling into last place behind vomit color.

We moved through the pink and purple archway and walked through a large room with four bag ladies sitting at a small table playing a game that had been built into the piece of furniture. The table whirred and flashed as they quickly hit colored squares in its top.

Lincoln ignored them and walked to a compudoor ahead of us and said a few words into the small speaker to the side of it. Apparently he said the right thing; the door whipped open so quickly that it just seemed to disappear.

Lincoln, the two bag ladies, and I stepped in and the door zipped shut behind us. I decided to be sure I wasn't standing too close to it next time it closed—I figured it might be easy to discover bits of yourself standing on both sides of it.

The interior of the chamber we stepped into was one big, hideous pink mirror with tiny veins running through it making it look like the inside of some living thing. The walls, ceiling, and floor were one continuous, seamless, pinkish mirror except for three doorways and the back of the room, which was all glass. Beyond the glass was a panoramic view of the sports field and the giant screen on the opposite side of the stadium, which allowed those in the stands to see close-ups of the field.

Upholstered swivel chairs were arranged in front of the glass with small tables between them. Each table was piled high with trays of fruit.

All the chairs were empty except for the largest one. Seated in it, looking down on the playing field far below us, was the mass of fat and flesh that was Sammy Dobrynin. I knew he was overweight but his pictures do him a disservice. He weighs at least twice as much as he appears to in the pictures. He was dressed in what looked like a pink sheet and had a garland of leaves around his greasy hair. Typical, everyday Nero get-up.

He slowly turned a blubbery face toward us. "Just in time for the game, Mr. Lincoln," his high feminine-sounding voice said. The flesh under his chin bounced about long after he'd quit talking. He rotated his chair around to face us. "Nothing like a good game of football to get the blood to boiling." He looked at me, "And how about you? Did you come to see the game?"

"I lost interest in it when they substituted clone giants for the robots," I said.

"Oh, come on!" he said and made a hoglike grunt. "When the defenders use their bats . . . all that blood is *so* exciting." He held up a hand that looked like a chunk of meat with sausages attached to it, and a young person of dubious sex came running forward from a corner of the room with a large platter of food. The "boy" had his skin dyed pink and was dressed only in a loin-cloth; pink sequins were glued over each of his nipples.

Dobrynin's oily fingers grubbed through the food and extracted half a chicken from the pile. "Excuse me, but we boys have to keep up our figures . . ."

In an age of no-cal foods and anti-fat pills, Dobrynin was going to give obesity a bad name, I thought. He patted his servant on the behind as the young man left. After slurping down a large greasy bit of chicken and spitting a bone on the floor, he spoke with a singsong rhythm, "Mr.

Lincolnnnnn—you haven't introduuuuuuced—us—'' He bat-
ted his eyes at me.

"Excuse me," Lincoln half bowed. "This is Phil Hunter,
the man that invented the antigravity rods."

"Ohhhh. So you're the naughty boy that's been giving
us so much trouble . . . ohhhh. Here come the teams. Sit
down, you two," he motioned us to the seats beside him.
Lincoln sat down, I remained up so I could beat a hasty
retreat if I needed to. And I wanted to stay out of the fat
old fruit's reach.

The ball games are just as awful as you hear. The giant
screen across from us allowed the fans—who had packed
the stadium—to see close-ups from cameras located all
around the stadium. The game started out with the usual
animal sacrifices to the players and ended with the sacrifice of the head cheer leader. She might have been an
android, and certainly seemed to have walked toward the
killer bot without coercion, but the blood and writhing
looked pretty real on the screen. It was all I could do to
keep from throwing up. I averted my eyes and tried not to
listen to her amplified screams and the roaring of the fans.

Finally, the preliminary sacrifices and fanfare were over
and the ten-foot-tall players in their chrome armor came
tromping onto the field. After the playing of the World
Anthem, the game began.

I'd already seen more of the game than I cared to.

I casually strolled around to get some idea what we were
up against. Assuming that Nikki had made it in and was
one of the two bag ladies, we only had one guard to
contend with in the room. And the three servant boys
stood about waiting for signals from Dobrynin; were they
dangerous? Could be, even though they looked harmless, I
decided. There didn't seem to be any sort of monitoring
equipment. And the room seemed to be thoroughly
soundproofed; the four bag ladies' noisy game in the front
room couldn't be heard in Dobrynin's room and the sounds
of the sports going on outside seemed to be piped in
through a speaker.

In addition to the entrance, which had a bag lady on
either side of it (one of which I hoped was Nikki), there
were doors on either side of the room. One was open and I

could see the wall-to-wall pink fur bed that filled the room beyond. No way I was going in there. The other door was closed. I fooled for a moment with a piece of pear that I picked off a platter of food, then walked toward the door as I munched on the juicy morsel.

Dobrynin did have good food, if you could keep the surroundings from turning your stomach.

As I neared the door, one of the boys quickly skipped over to block my way. "Sorry," his almost masculine voice said.

"Uh . . . I'm looking for a rest room," I whispered to him.

"That's the communications room in there," he whispered back and put a friendly hand on my shoulder. "Dobrynin has us use that urn in the corner. He thinks it's a good joke. I'm sure you'd really make a hit if you just went over there and—"

"That's OK. I can wait." What a disgusted bunch of maggots, I thought. Time to get the ball rolling, I decided. If Nikki had made it into the room with us. If she hadn't, I was hoping to leave quietly.

Time to test out the bag ladies. I whistled the opening bars of Beethoven's Fifth.

One of the bag ladies scratched her head and adjusted her mask. Provided I hadn't just managed the world's worst coincidence, I thought, Nikki made it in.

Now it was time for signal two: I whistled a few bars of the *2112 Overture*. The music triggered a response from Lincoln. "Time for a little chat, Mr. Dobrynin," he said as he flipped off a switch in front of Dobrynin. The sound of the game being piped into the room was suddenly cut off.

"What the hell're you doing?" Dobrynin said, flipping the switch back on, and the sounds of the fan again gushed in. "Am I going to have to spank you?"

Lincoln reached over and switched the sound off again. He paused a moment in the abrupt silence, then ripped the control pedestal off the floor and hurled it across the room where it shattered the mirrored wall. That takes care of that, I thought.

The bag lady next to Nikki raised her gun; Nikki raised hers a little faster. The barrel of Nikki's shotgun lined up with the unarmored area of the bag lady's neck. The discharge sounded quite loud in the room.

The bag lady turned slightly, stumbled, then fell, fast asleep with the stun chemical coursing through her veins.

One of the boys pulled out a knife—how he'd hidden it on his person is beyond me—and stepped toward Nikki.

"Do you really want to do that?" I asked with the Beretta in my hand.

I guess he did since he threw the knife at me. Fortunately, his athletic skills were about as good as his looks and the blade went careening past me and shattered the mirror behind me. Dobrynin was going to have some major redecorating to do.

Nikki put the knife thrower down for his nap and quickly aced the other two boys as well. I decided to ask her where she'd learned to shoot so well if and when we got out of our predicament.

Taking his part as a leader of the world to heart, Sammy Dobrynin fell on the floor and had a tantrum.

And I don't exaggerate.

It was a real chew-the-rug, scream-and-holler, curse-and-threaten, hold-your-breath-and-turn-purple tantrum. If we could have sold tickets, we might have retired right there.

Lincoln and I started laughing and the show came to an abrupt halt.

"You . . . you dirty boys," he sputtered as he got up onto his chubby knees.

"Why don't you just shut up, you tub of lard, and listen to what Mr. Hunter has to say," Lincoln said.

Another tantrum. But this one didn't last as long.

"Are you ready to listen, fatso," Lincoln asked. I decided he had missed his calling as a diplomat. I also figured he'd hate himself when he realized that we'd filled him full of chemicals in order to get him to bring us in and insult his boss. No doubt he'd be on the run after this. Sammy didn't look too forgiving.

"What do you want?" he said as he eased his frame into his chair. His face glowed a furious red.

"Well," I said, "I need to talk to you. We need to have an understanding."

"Tell me what you want so I can get back to my game."

"Yeah, we don't want to let the state of the world interfere with our ball game," I said. "We want you to agree to quit hounding us and to release the antigravity technology to the public."

"You don't beat around the bush, Mr., uh . . . whatever your name is. Just what do you stand to gain from that?"

"My life. I want to be left alone."

"And just what would I gain?"

"Dobrynin, you get all the wealth created by cheap energy."

He laughed. "What makes you think I need more wealth?"

"You must. Otherwise you'd quit trying to get rid of me and my new invention. But I don't aim to compete with your monopoly. I figure that once you start turning out the rods, all of us will benefit. And you'll get even richer. Just leave me alone and my secret is yours."

Again Dobrynin laughed. And laughed. He all but fell out of his chair. Finally, he wiped the tears out of his eyes and spoke, "You fool. I already have the formula. You don't understand how things work. Why do you think all our new technology isn't used?

"Did you ever wonder why we haven't circled the Earth with solar cells and beamed microwave energy down to Earth? Or how about fusion power? If we were on the ball, your antigravity would hardly make a dent in things. Why are there steel shortages when we could mine the Moon? Did you know we've closed our operations down there?"

I said nothing.

"Want to know why?"

I nodded.

"Because the operations would be successful. We have to keep all the peons poor. It isn't easy to keep control of all the naughty girls and boys on this planet."

"He's crazy," I said to Lincoln.

"No. And he isn't alone in his thinking. The industrial cartel agrees with him. More or less. Listen to what he's saying. It makes sense," Lincoln said.

"Yes," Dobrynin continued. "Think about history. When do you have revolts and uprisings?"

"Whenever the people don't have enough. When they're oppressed."

"Wrong, wrong, wrong, wrong, wrong," Dobrynin whined. "If you'd study history—really study history, not this tripe we have them telling the school brats—you'll discover that revolts and turmoil occur when people start to get a higher standard of living. Or when they see their neighbors getting it and they aren't. During real times of hardship—the dark ages, the depressions, hyper-inflation—people knuckle under. They look to their government to help them. They become beggars—not fighters."

"And that's what you want?"

"You bet. By slowly lowering the standard of living, by letting them expect a price rise on their utilities, we gradually gain control of everything. As long as they sit at home and watch the 3V or come to my games, I have the power and we all have peace. Since we started manipulating the government, there hasn't been anything other than border squabbles and an occasional terrorist act."

"But . . ." I didn't know what to say.

"You throw in a monkey wrench with antigravity now and everyone is going to want a flying vehicle; but not everyone can have one. The skies can't hold them all. And if even a few have them, my rocket system will go broke. Everyone is going to expect cheap energy; what happens to the people who work in the power plants? Are they going to want to be on the public fares while their neighbors continue to work? No. We'll just have more friction. Those who've lost their jobs to your new technology won't be able to keep up with the others. We'll have protests and, finally, riots. And who finally loses? The government. And who runs the government?"

"The people," I said. And felt instantly foolish.

Lincoln and Dobrynin both laughed.

"You must think you're in the good old days. No wonder you want to give power away. No, we can't let that happen. Now why don't you leave and let me watch my games?"

He turned back and watched the games. Lincoln sat

still, having come to the end of his program. I stood and
fumed for ten minutes, wondering if I might still be able to
do something else. I hadn't expected to be able to reason
with Dobrynin; yet I had hoped that perhaps we could get
everyone off our backs so that we could go about our
work. And I had hoped against hope that we'd be able to
get my antigravity technology released to those on Earth
who really needed it to raise their standard of living.

But we had all half expected a response similar to
Dobrynin's.

It was time to use our drug kit to program Dobrynin.

20

"Nikki," I said, "get out your drug kit. Nikki?" She was nowhere around. I gave the room another look. "Nikki!"

"Don't panic, Phil," she said from the room I'd tried to get into earlier. "Just a minute."

A few moments later she entered the room, "I've been playing with Dobrynin's computers. I could see you weren't going to reach a gentleman's agreement." She'd taken off her bag lady mask and helmet/wig since it was so warm where we were.

"No. Old Slime Ball's theory of history won't allow it." I looked at him a moment. He was watching the violent game and drooling. I turned back to Nikki. "I think we're going to have to help him see things our way."

Nikki handed me her shotgun and took the drug kit out of the large pocket in her bag-lady uniform.

Dobrynin was—I thought—sitting and watching the game. But he had been sneaking a peak, apparently. When the kit came out, he screamed, "No!" He seemed to know what we had in mind for him. I looked over and saw him standing, his face red with rage.

Dobrynin was the first fat man I'd really ever seen. Yes, they do have them in the 3V's but we all know those are just actors in fat suits. Maybe even a little synthaskin. But not real flesh-and-blood, honest-to-goodness blubber.

So I didn't realize how fast a fat man can move when he needs to. I just assumed he was like a whale on land. Not so. While Nikki was looking into the kit, Dobrynin's obese fingers grabbed a tray of fruit as his body lurched forward and he threw it.

The edge of the tray collided with Nikki's temple and she fell, dropping the black medical case. I watched as Nikki, the tray, a rainbow of fruit, and the kit did a complicated ballet with gravity and dropped in a tangle. The case and fruit hit first, then Nikki landed on them. The tray continued past her and shattered another section of the mirrored room.

I was furious and afraid Nikki might be seriously injured.

"Good-night, you fat old—" I said and pumped a stun slug into Dobrynin. He blinked in surprise. I suppose he didn't realize that they were only stun shells. I pumped three more into him figuring anyone with that much mass to him might need an extra-large dose. He just stood there. I got ready to fire again and he toppled face down into a bowl of fruit on the table next to his chair. The table wobbled a moment and then collapsed under the enormous weight.

Lincoln looked at me. Our programming of him had made it impossible for him to do anything once the action started but I decided not to take any chances. I fired at him, missed, and fired again twice, hitting his body.

"But—" he said.

"Sorry, but you're not really on our team. You're only as good as the chemicals we trained you with."

He toppled over without protest. I laid the shotgun down and knelt beside Nikki who was struggling to get up.

"Are you OK?"

"Yeah. I'm going to have a whale of a headache." She laughed. "That's probably fitting, isn't it." She turned the medical kit over. It was a mess of liquid, fruit, and splinters of glass. "Now what?"

"Now, we get out of here the best way we can and get to Jake. We'll figure out another plan later. If we were smart, we'd kill Dobrynin and end one of the world's major problems. But I know that neither of us can do that."

"And someone else would just take his place."

"Right."

"Wrong," Nikki said.

"You're not going to kill—"

"No. I did better than that. I was able to get into the computer and mess things up royally. It'd been left on so I didn't need any access codes. I just created a major sellout of World Energy stocks. Also, I created a few press releases. The company is going to make an announcement of your discovery and how you made it. The population is going to be primed for cheap energy, space exploration, and you-name-it in a few minutes."

I swallowed and tried to let it sink in. "Are you sure that . . . will it . . . what?"

"Never at a loss for words, Phil." She grabbed me and gave me a quick kiss. "Now let's get out of here."

"Right. But how? We can't drug all of them out there. Maybe you can get out as a bag lady again. I could be the prisoner and you could . . ."

"I have a better idea. See that bag lady sleeping on the floor? If I can dress up, then so can—"

"Now wait a minute. I'll never get dressed up like a bag lady."

I soon had her clothes on; it was either that or one of the cute pink G-strings the boys were wearing. I figured the bag lady outfit was more masculine.

We calmly walked out the door and let it close behind us. We marched down the hall and caught the elevator without being stopped. We had to get away because all hell would break loose in the stadium in five minutes.

And yes, in case you haven't guessed it, that was the game that the crowd tore down the stadium when the game was canceled and all the power shut off. It was added to the many losses World Energy totaled up that day. If you'd ever met Dobrynin, I'm sure you would have done the same favor for him.

We had little trouble sneaking out to the Miami rocket port that afternoon. The big problem was whether or not there would be anything left of Miami when Jake finally got there. I guess we underestimated the love of fans for their sports.

21

We managed to flag down a taxi just outside of the stadium elevator; inside the high walls of the stadium, we could hear the cursing and hollering as the power went down. The dozens of bag ladies around Dobrynin's elevator went scurrying about doing tasks as we opened the taxi doors.

"Where to, ladies?" the tiny little man behind the wheel asked unaware of the impending riot going on nearby.

I slid into the seat behind him. "The rocket port," I said. Then cleared my throat and tried it again in my best falsetto, "The rocket port."

"No," Nikki said from her side of the seat as she slammed the door.

The driver turned around. It was only then that I saw that he was standing on the seat, "Come on ladies, I don't have all day."

Nikki was studying a computer printout she'd produced from her pocket and spoke without looking up, "Take us to the prison. And don't get smart or we'll cut a couple more inches off you."

"OK, OK. No need to get upset," he said. He turned around and grabbed a control stick to shift the vehicle into gear and spun away from the curb.

As we accelerated away from the stadium, I turned to see if anyone was following us. Amid the flurry of bag ladies, no one seemed to be even looking our way. As I watched, a large section of the stadium's plastic siding was hurled to the ground from above by a group of fans. One seemed to have forgotten to let go of it and fell to his death and managed to crush a number of those who were still waiting to buy tickets to a game that wasn't going to be finished due to a lack of power.

I turned around and settled into the seat and—as we jumped up onto the curb to miss a large police riot truck barreling toward the stadium—decided to fasten my seat belt.

Like the driver of the limo, our taxi driver didn't seem too concerned about the pedestrians. Though he did slow down to let an old man get out of the way he was quick to explain, "Those old codgers put big dents in my car. Got to be careful."

As if to make up for it, he clipped a monopod, spilling the rider.

I leaned over and whispered to Nikki, "Why are we going to the prison? That should be where we're trying not to go!"

She handed me the sheet.

"Terminate" it read across the top in large letters. The date was tomorrow, I decided after a little thought (so much had been going on, it was hard to keep track of the days). I read the list of names that didn't mean much to me. Then the names started to ring bells. Scientists.

Then a member of my antigravity research team.

"Where'd you get this?"

"From Dobrynin's computer."

If one team member had survived the attempts to hide our secret, had others? I wondered.

The names were in alphabetical order. I started checking up and down the list. All but one of the team and myself were listed.

Then they were still alive. But not for long if something wasn't done.

"Couldn't you have released them through the computer?"

Nikki shook her head, "I tried. But such an order needs to have personal authorization."

"Dobrynin's personal authorization?"

"None other. I didn't think he looked like he'd be interested last time I saw him. . . ."

"OK, but . . . do you have a plan?"

"No. I figured you could come up with something."

"Sure . . . why don't we just wing it? Our best laid plans don't seem to be having such a great track record these days."

"Look here," she pointed at the name on the list. "Recognize her name?"

I shook my head.

"That just happens to be one of the top bot designers in this hemisphere. Her name is what caught my eye when I happened to see the list by the computer."

"Executing these people must be Dobrynin's way of helping to keep things stagnant. Stupid ninny."

"Here it is," the driver said as he screeched to a halt and threw us up against the back of his seat.

"What do you think?" Nikki asked. "It doesn't look too formidable."

I looked at the small concrete archway of the prison. The entrance looked like it was all door and no building. It didn't look big. "We're here. Let's see if we can do something."

We got out.

"Hey. How about my pay?"

Nikki clicked off the safety of her shotgun and pointed it in the driver's direction. "Wait here."

"Yes, ma'am," the short driver said with a gulp.

"And don't try any tricks. We have your license number and can track you down."

The tiny man gulped again.

"Just a minute," I said. "We'll be needing, uh," I looked at the list and did some quick figuring, "some more transportation if we succeed." I turned toward the driver, "Get ten more taxis here. Get them here in a hurry."

"Uh. Well—"

"Dobrynin will pay ten times the normal fares," I lied.

"OK, they'll be here in a couple of minutes," he said grabbing his talkie.

Nothing like greed, I thought. At the same time I felt guilty. I decided that if I got back out of the prison, I'd get him some sort of extra pay after this was over. In his own way, the little taxi driver was as much a victim of Dobrynin's crimes as we were.

We ran across the long gray plastic walk leading to the

prison entrance, which was built into the concrete dike that ringed Miami.

"Replace the stun shells with standard flechettes," I told Nikki. "The delay it takes before the stun shells take effect could get us killed."

"Yeah, that's a good idea. I'm about out of the special shells, anyway."

I checked my shotgun as she slipped a new magazine into hers. As we stepped on the threshold plate, the huge door opened, then closed as we stepped into a small room. A large camera swiveled toward us and trained its lasers on us.

"Business?" a voice said.

"We've come to pick up the prisoners for Dobrynin," Nikki said.

I hoped she knew what she was doing and quietly snapped the safety off my shotgun in case we needed to try to take out the laser.

The door ahead of us opened and we walked forward and stepped into the waiting elevator. As it sank down, I saw why there'd been no prison building to see from the front. It was because the prison was underwater.

The elevator was clear plastic and slowly dropped us one story below the surface of the ocean. We watched as fish performed their acrobatics outside the elevator. Around us, the bottom of the ocean showed a wealth of green life amid the ruins of Old Miami. Though the battering of the waves and the caustic action of the salt water and sea life had taken their toll, it was still possible to make out the streets and blocks that extended out from the area. Several rusty hulks of cars stood in the streets, as if waiting to again be driven toward the abandoned homes.

Far in the distance, a large sea farm was crawling through the violent, oxygen-rich waves that rolled over the ruins of the city. The farm's surface extended as far as we could see toward the northeast of the prison.

The prison itself extended only a short distance in a fork out from the central transparent bubble into which the elevator opened. There were few cells; there were many capital offenses, and punishment was often carried out without a court hearing.

Each cell along the prison hallway was a small dome on the ocean floor, among the decaying ruins. The various cells were interconnected by clear walkways laid on the floor of the ocean. As the waves rolled above us, the prison domes swayed slightly. There seemed to be no artificial lights; light filtered into the area in bright patterns of yellow, green, and blue from the bright shimmering mirrored surface above us where the ocean and air met.

As we stepped out of the elevator, we were met by the damp stench of sweat and urine. We looked around for a moment then walked toward the large desk in the center of the dome. An old man sat behind a stained, white plastic desk. His large, sunken eyes inspected us closely.

"What prisoners are you talking about?" he said, breaking the quiet of the room.

"We've come to pick up these prisoners," Nikki said, sliding the paper we'd brought with us.

He looked at the paper without picking it up, then frowned, making more wrinkles on his leathery face. He punched a button on the desktop and inspected the display of names that sprang onto the monitor in front of him.

He shook his head and snapped the display off then rubbed a hand over his bald head, "Why can't you people get things straight? I got the order to release these people just a while ago and—as are my orders—requested the written authorization. And never got it. You'll have to wait until I get it."

"It was sent over ten minutes ago," Nikki said.

"Let me call." He removed a talkie from the surface of the desk where it had appeared to be part of the flat surface. He spoke his number then listened a moment. "Nothing," he said. "What in the world's . . . ."

I didn't wait around anymore. I slapped him up the side of the head with the barrel of my shotgun and he fell over his desktop in a really fine Rip Van Winkle imitation.

"Now what," Nikki said.

I shrugged.

"I was hoping you had an idea when you tucked him in."

"Well, there's not much else to do. Let's see if we can get into the cells."

We ran toward the metal door leading to the prison

cells. I dilated it open and came face to face with a bag lady.

She looked at me a moment, then stared past me. I knew she saw the warden's body and she knew I knew. We both pulled up our weapons at the same instant and fired. I missed and hers connected.

Her gun was of a type I'd never seen before: a short-barreled handgun with a heavy, lead-pellet-filled projectile about ten centimeters across. The huge slug caught me in the chest and knocked the wind out of me, causing me to keel over as I tried to breathe. Only the ballistic armor incorporated into the bag lady outfit kept me from greater harm.

The bag lady quickly tried to reload her weapon as Nikki jumped past me and fired; Nikki's shot missed. I fired again from my knees.

This time I connected with the lethal flechette load of the shotgun. The bag lady fell with a large, fist-sized hole in her chest.

I gasped for air a moment and stood up. The first thing that captured my attention was the sound of water.

"What?" I said.

"That's why she had such an ineffective weapon," Nikki said, pointing to the streams of water gushing through the plastic of the hallway. "Anything else is too dangerous. Your first flechette load as well as mine punctured the plastic."

"Damn. I wonder if it will hold up?"

As if to answer my question, a large chunk of plastic broke free from one of the tiny streams of water and a torrent of water gushed in. Moments later, the other hole widened to admit more water.

"Come on," I said. "We don't have much time. We've got to get the prisoners out of here or they'll drown."

We splashed down the passage to the fork in the hallway. "I'll take the left," Nikki said.

I dashed down the right. I was glad to see that most of the cells were empty. I stopped at the first occupied cell I came to. I tried to open it. It appeared to have an electric lock of some type. I heard a shot down the hall. Trouble?

"You OK, Nikki?" I yelled over the racket the water was making.

"Blasted the lock," Nikki yelled.

Might as well try it, I thought. I motioned the young man inside the cell to stand back and placed the muzzle of the shotgun on the plastic lock while trying to aim downward so any flechettes that went through the lock wouldn't harm the prisoner or puncture the plastic bubble of his cell.

I pulled the trigger and the lock exploded apart. My ears rang.

"Get going," I told him as I pushed the heavy plastic door back, "the prison is flooding."

He didn't need any prompting. He scooped up a small bag of belongings off the floor and jumped out of the cell and sloshed toward the elevator.

The water was now ankle deep. I ran to the next cells and had soon blasted eight more open freeing three men and two women (none of whom I knew) and also freeing three of my team members who—to my surprise—didn't recognize me. Then I remembered my bag lady get up. I didn't take time for reunions but just ordered them to the door and hoped they didn't try to attack me since I looked like one of the old hags they had no doubt learned to hate.

That completed the release of everyone on the wing. The water was now knee deep and rising rapidly.

I half waded, half swam toward the fork. "Nikki, you almost finished?"

She came splashing up with two bedraggled women, "Yeah. That's it. Let's get out of here."

We made our way to the main chamber. I looked through the clear dome and water at the load of prisoners getting out of the elevator above us. I scooped up the little warden who was still draped across his desk, the water lapping at its top. The elevator was coming back down for the five of us when the power went off.

The water was chest high and the elevator was frozen halfway down.

"We'll never get out," one of the women said.

It looked like she was right.

22

"Listen," I said over the gushing roar of the water, "we could last a long time if we had to by getting up to the top of this chamber. It's airtight and the dome top would create an air pocket. Someone would eventually come and rescue us."

Maybe. It didn't sound all that reassuring.

"It'd be better to get out," Nikki said.

Especially since no one will probably be coming to help, I thought. I didn't say that since I didn't want to panic everyone. "Yeah. It would be better if we could get out on our own. The only way up is the elevator. So let's see if we can get up the elevator shaft."

It sounded easy; it wouldn't be, I thought.

The plastic was as slick as only the new plastics can be. Like trying to get a hold of a greased stick of frozen luber. The first order of business was to cut some hand-holds into the plastic.

"Stand back," I said, throwing off my bag woman mask and hat so I could see better.

Some great sage in the dark and distant past said that guns were only tools. So far that theory had held up; the shotgun had worked well in opening the prison locks. Now I was going to test it out as a chisel. I fired three times at the tube of the elevator. The projectiles chewed three jagged holes, fortunately without punching more holes in the dome beyond the elevator shaft.

Each hole was about a third of a meter higher than the next. They were the perfect size for climbing, I discovered as I pulled myself up on them and was nearly against the base of the elevator.

I placed the muzzle of my gun against the clear elevator floor above me and fired, creating another hole. I quickly fired another six shots around it, trying to ignore the splinters of plastic that threatened to put out my eyes as they splattered from the impact of the flechettes. The holes made, I used the gun for a lever and broke out the area around the shots until a man-sized hole was created over my head.

I tossed the shotgun into the elevator, held the jagged edge around the hole, and scrambled through it. I turned and reached down toward the two women and Nikki who held up the floating warden, below me. "Who's next?"

One of the women climbed up and I grabbed her hand and pulled her through. She sat on the floor as I pulled up the second woman. The warden was the tough one. The water was now up higher than Nikki was but she had a foot on the lower hole I'd punched in the plastic and now half lifted the floating warden out of the water as I grabbed the fabric of his jacket.

"He looked little, must have gold bars in his pockets," I gasped. One of the women in the elevator grabbed him and together we hauled him up through the hole. Nikki scrambled up behind him and brushed her wet hair back out of her face.

"Now what?" one of the women asked.

"Just blast some more holes," the other said.

"Not that easy," Nikki spoke. "The shaft is next to the water now. Any shots at the wall of the tube will bring in water. It only worked below because we were in the bubble of the chamber."

I thought a moment, then blasted another large hole in the roof of the elevator. "At least we can climb a little closer to the surface," I yelled. Nikki fired several shots in the same area and we soon had carved out a large hole above us. I pushed my shotgun up into it and broke out the few sharp points left in the crude circular opening.

The ceiling of the elevator was too high to reach and the water that was now bubbling up around my knees made it impossible to jump.

"Let me boost you," I said to the smaller of the two women.

The water was up to our hips by the time she and the other woman had scrambled up. Nikki and I lifted the warden up to them. We nearly dropped him but finally his limp body was pulled through.

"OK, Nikki, you're next."

"But . . ."

"Come on."

She put her foot into my hands and was pulled up by the outstretched arms of the women above her.

I handed my gun up to them then tried to jump up to their arms and succeeded only in falling down into the water. I came sputtering back up and took a deep breath of air, lost my footing, and dropped back into the water. I came up again spitting out salt water. My eyes burned and my wet clothes seemed to weigh a ton. I tore at the release of my ballistic vest so I wouldn't be dragged under so easily again.

When I finally got the water out of my eyes, I could see the warden's belt they'd lowered to me. I got a tight hold on it and the three above me pulled my heavy carcass up until I was even with the hole. Holding myself with one hand on the belt, I pulled my body up in a way I've never been able to do since then and got my elbow over the jagged edge of the plastic hole. The three women pulled on my hands and arms until I popped onto the top of the elevator with them.

We were in a fix, I thought as I looked at the smooth sides of the tube and the four meters or so still to go to the edge of ground level of the shaft.

"Could we get on your shoulders?" one of the women asked me.

I thought a moment as the water lapped at my ankles. "We'd better try something." I leaned against the side of the shaft, "Go on. Climb up if you can."

She scrambled up my back, managing to nearly claw my bag lady skirt off and threatening to flatten my skull as she booted herself up the final few inches. "Can't reach it!" she called down.

"Help!" she hollered. I realized she was trying to contact someone outside the elevator shaft rather than calling to us. She called three more times, then lost her balance and slid off my shoulders and clawed her way down into the knee-deep water.

Things looked bad.

"Shall we try blasting holes in the sides of the shaft?" Nikki asked.

"Guess so, better than drowning like a bunch of rats without even—"

"Hello down there?" a voice came from above us.

"Help!" the woman next to me screamed again, nearly putting out my eardrum.

"Hang on."

I expected them to toss down a rope or something. Instead, a moment later the whole elevator started to rise. It jerked and stopped, then slowly inched its way up. The water was now at our necks and slowly gained on us even as we went up. Nikki held the warden's face above water and I held up the short woman as the water started to reach our mouths.

"Hurry up!" I blubbered.

A face looked down at us from above. It disappeared a moment, then returned. "Hold on, we're having to raise the elevator by hand."

The water was too high for us.

We started coughing as it overtook us, rising over our noses. Then the elevator jerked. The water dropped and we struggled for air, only to have the water suddenly bubble up over our heads.

I pushed up the short woman struggling beside me. Even if I can't breathe, I thought, at least I can buy her a few more minutes. As soon as I had pushed her up, her weight was lifted from me and I felt her thrashing feet graze my scalp. I floated over to Nikki and boosted her up also.

Again, she was suddenly gone.

My lungs felt as if they were bursting. I exhaled underwater then bobbed up and grabbed a breath of air then searched for the other woman but couldn't find her. I opened my eyes under the water and looked around. Then I squinted downward and saw her below me. Somehow she had fallen through the hole in the top of the elevator and was below it.

She had her eyes closed tightly and couldn't see to find her way through the hole. She had panicked—as anyone probably would—and was clawing at the top of the elevator below me; she couldn't find the opening.

I floundered around trying to dive down and finally succeeded in reaching the hole with my fingers. Grasping its edge, I pulled myself down; my ears popped as water filled them. I reached through the hole and got a good handful of the woman's hair and pulled her toward the opening. She was thrashing around as I lifted her up through the hole. She managed to hit me in the nose and then relaxed as she passed out.

I grabbed her limp body around the waist. My lungs felt as if they'd ruptured as I kicked off from the top of the elevator toward the sparkling surface of the water.

As we broke the surface I passed out.

23

By the time Nikki had emptied the brine from my lungs and managed to pump in enough air to revive me, we were halfway to the rocket port in the fleet of taxis our little driver had rounded up for us.

Unfortunately, his good work was rewarded with only a "thank-you." Our driver was on the warpath when we couldn't pay him; I thought maybe he would chew off my kneecap before we got him settled down.

When I told him who I was and wrote him an IOU, he finally looked me right in the face and said, "Hey, wait a minute. You really are that Hunter guy. I saw the newscast while you were at the prison."

"Yeah. Well, what we'd like to—"

"I think I like your hair better the way it was."

"Yeah . . . well . . . I'll make good on what we owe you if you give me your address and—"

"No need," he said tearing up the IOU. "Just give me a ride in the first spaceship you build with your rods. I've always wanted to get into space but I'm too short."

"That probably won't be—"

"And, buddy," he said as he jumped onto the seat of his cab, "if I were you, I'd quit wearing your dress in public. You've got to think of the image you're projecting."

As I stood there, I took quite a ribbing from the lab team and Nikki about my soggy dress. I felt like I might have been better off leaving them all in the prison.

We finally located a vending machine at the port and Nikki and I both dialed up some plastic unisex coveralls.

The prisoners did likewise and in a few moments, we were outfitted in regular attire and our prison uniforms and dresses were discarded down a garbage chute. By the time we'd purchased new outfits for everyone, Nikki and I had run through all the change in the pockets of our bag lady outfits. I decided to write a note to Dobrynin telling him to pay his bag ladies better so there'd be more money to spend next time we rolled one.

At any rate, we now looked like paupers rather than prisoners or wayward bag ladies, and I was no longer self-conscious about my outfit.

"Phil," Tom Barrel, one of my lab group, said as he gripped my arm in his muscled hand, "we gave you quite a ribbing, but we'd like to say thanks for getting us out of there. They were ready to—"

"No thanks is necessary guys," I said. "I know that you'd have done the same for me. And Nikki did most of the work anyway. Just quit talking about that crazy outfit and we'll call it even."

Everyone laughed and we got on to other things. The looks of gratitude on the faces of those Nikki and I had rescued were all the thanks we needed.

With the problems at the stadium, no one in charge seemed to be too concerned about the escape of sixteen political prisoners even if they knew that everyone hadn't remained in their cells when the prison flooded. The warden—whom we'd left sleeping soundly on the floor of one of the cabs—probably wouldn't be saying anything for another two or three hours.

Nevertheless, things were tense since we had several major problems. The worst was what we were going to do for transportation. With the sixteen people we'd released from the prison and Nikki and myself, even when Jake came, we had only a ride for three people. Though we could stack everyone into the van like a load of bots, the gravity rods would put too much stress on them if we flew the van, and if we didn't, getting from Miami to Jake's place in Texas would take forever.

Since none of us had money or cards, there was no way to purchase a ride on a rocket. And we wouldn't dare to try to commandeer a ride—it would be too easy for ground control to change the destination or even blow up the rocket. Hijacking rides was a thing they did in the good old days. Jake usually carried some money, but it was doubtful that'd he'd have enough to pay for more than two or three passengers' fares.

Another problem of more general interest was that it looked like Nikki might have been too successful in dismantling Dobrynin's empire. In fact, as I watched the small 3V in the waiting room at the port, I thought we might have succeeded in putting the whole planet into a neo-dark age. The announcement of the discovery of antigravity and the dissolution of World Energy made quite an impact with the world stock market falling to record lows before being prematurely closed for the week. Adding to the confusion was the spontaneous walk-off from jobs worldwide as people headed toward the nearest 3V. (The French were the worst about this. They threw what looked like a nationwide celebration boasting that "Hunter" was actually a corruption of an old French name—that had to make my ancestors somewhere rotate in their abodes.)

Rioting broke out in Britain, Japan, and most of Africa, while an interview with the president of the Flat Earth Society revealed that they thought I should be drawn and quartered. I made a note to put them at the bottom of my speaking engagement list.

But when the 3V news specials started wheeling out the usual tired experts who explained why antigravity wasn't possible and/or what impact the technology could have on our society and economy with the usual (ho-hum) graphs and file footage, I could see that my research would be received in the usual shortsighted, business-as-usual way.

And that was good.

I suspect that many people would have gone into shock if they'd realized that almost all types of travel and energy production would shortly become obsolete and that the whole solar system could now be used for raw materials.

Fortunately, in the confusion, police and bag ladies at the rocket port were all busy leaving to sort things out at the stadium. All of our group just stuck close to the crowd milling around the 3V, while Nikki and I kept our shotguns hidden but ready in case we got into a real confrontation.

We took up our guard duty in a spot that allowed us to watch both the 3V and the parking lot where we hoped Jake would be showing up shortly. Night fell as a formation of fighter planes went screaming overhead. Apparently authorities had decided to stop the rioting around the stadium in a hurry; a brilliant column of fire soon rose over the stadium area as the planes dropped their loads of napalm. After that, things calmed down since there probably weren't many rioters left.

Nothing like a little urban renewal to solve clashes, I thought.

"There's the van," Nikki leaned over and whispered to me and nodded toward the parking lot.

I stood up and addressed our small group. "OK, everyone stay here while we go and talk to Jake and try to sort everything out. We'll be right back."

Jake smiled as he stepped through the autodoors into the rocket station and we met him.

"Boy, you guys really split it wide open."

"Yeah, I just hope we didn't do too good a job," Nikki said.

"No, looks like it's going over pretty well," he said, giving Nikki a big hug. "It's nice that you got the credit for your work, too, Phil. You need to get a newer picture of yourself. For the news people. That skin cut hairdo looks wild."

"Yeah, that's my college graduation photo. Apparently, that's all they've been able to dig up. Look, we have a problem."

We briefly explained to him about our extra sixteen passengers.

Jake chuckled. "Money is no problem. My nephew's proving to be quite a trader. Should've turned the business over to him sooner, I guess. Had a customer lined up for some of the industrial stuff we brought back from the Moon. Here," he took a large wad of bills from his jacket pocket and peeled off two large bills, "this ought to cover it."

"Wow, I guess so," I said. "We'll have them take a

rocket to Houston then we'll ferry them over to your place, if that's OK.''

"Sure," Jake said. "We could use the extra help to get the antigravity rods and stuff we brought back sorted out and into the machinery we've been planning on building. With the publicity you got today, we'd better get some things going for the press to see or we'll go down as the greatest hoaxers in history.''

Nikki and I got the money to the group and said our good-byes, then headed out to the parking lot with Jake.

"Guess we'll head after their rocket," I said.

"You guys better let me fly the van, you look pretty worn out,'' Jake said as we got nearer the van.

"We only look that way because we are," I said as we got in.

The rocket going back to Houston left only a half hour after Jake had arrived. Soon those we'd rescued were getting safely snuggled down in their rocket and we were waiting in the parking lot to follow them up.

We were slipping into our space suits (since the top of the arc of the flight after the rocket would take us into pretty thin air) when Jake said, "You know, I think I'd better use the rest room in the station. Just a minute, I'll be right back.''

I figured he must have gotten nervous kidneys thinking about how well he flew the van. He left and Nikki and I got our suits on and waited patiently.

Then we heard shooting.

We turned in our seats and saw a group of bag ladies run into the front of the rocket port building.

"Now what?" I asked. It could only be trouble.

We watched a moment and then saw the bag ladies marching Jake out in a small parade. There were nine of the look-alike bag ladies in front and two on either side dragged Jake—who appeared unconscious. Four more of the bag ladies brought up the rear.

"Oh no," Nikki said. "What shall we . . .''

"There are too many to try to fight," I said. We only had our two shotguns—which were about out of ammunition—and I'd lost my Beretta somewhere during the day's activities.

"Have you seen the rail gun?" I asked. "I did have it stowed in the van."

"No, but I haven't been in the back."

"Keep track of where they're headed." I got up and went back. The rail gun was still fastened to the side of the van. I removed it from its straps and brought it back forward.

"Well, we have a lot of overkill at least. This thing could take on a fighter plane. Where's Jake now?"

"They put him in that green car over there," Nikki pointed. "The ladies seem to be getting into the two cars ahead and the one behind the car they have him in."

"OK. We've got to stop them before they get too far. If they're in cars, they must be leaving the rocket port area. We could lose them in the city traffic, as crazy as it is. . . ."

"There's only the one road off the rocket port into Miami—"

"Right. If we hurry, we can head them off."

"But what will we do if we catch up with them?"

"This rail gun can take out a car. If I hit it right. We'll have to try to get the escort cars and cut the odds down to what we can handle with just the two of us."

Nikki jumped into the driver's seat, "Let me drive and you fire the rail gun, I don't know the slightest thing about it."

I decided not to tell her I didn't know anything about the rail gun either. Why do women always assume that men know all about weapons?

She put the van into gear and we raced toward the road. The bag ladies' caravan started at the same moment. We were all racing toward the road with a column of parked vehicles between the cars and our van.

As we moved down the poorly lit parking lot we were neck and neck with the cars. Then we inched ahead several car lengths. It looked like we might pull ahead when, halfway toward the entrance of the rocket port, a car pulled out of its parking space ahead of us, blocking our way as we hurtled forward. Nikki slammed on her brakes and we skidded toward the car.

We bashed into it with a resounding crumpling of metal. An angry giant jumped from the car.

"Sorry," I yelled to him as we backed away, "we've got a friend to rescue."

He hurled his hat at us and coated the warm Miami air with curses as Nikki reached the end of the long line of parked cars and turned the van around.

The bag ladies' cars were now at the end of the parking lot and they were turning onto the road that ran out over the dark ocean. The cars' taillights showed the only light other than the reflection of the burning stadium in the powerless city.

"OK, the only way to head them off is to fly," I said. "Get up some height so we don't crush anyone with our downward push."

We rose into the air. "What about the radar?"

"We'll have to risk it," I said as I fell back into the seat under the enormous acceleration of the car. We quickly pulled up alongside the cars, floating over the ocean to one side of the bridgelike roadway. Nikki had the lights off and no one in the cars seemed to be aware of us.

"Let's try dropping down over the lead car," I said. "The wash from our rods might be harsh enough to force them to stop."

That was an understatement. As we dropped down, the car faltered a moment, bouncing up and down on its shocks, and broke through the steel rail and went careening into the ocean with a tremendous splash. The car behind it either felt the effects of our passage or the driver panicked. In any event, it went crashing through the rail on the opposite side of the road and went splashing into the black water as well.

Nikki pulled up and put the van into a steep curve. I was slammed into the door, which popped open, and I nearly fell out before I grabbed the seat and held on for dear life.

"Let's try that on the rear car," Nikki yelled, ignoring the fact that I was about to drop on them like superman without the super.

"Yahhhhhhggggggg," I answered.

She ignored me and finished the turn as we wheeled behind the rear car and dropped down toward it as it sped along the road. I slammed the door shut and quickly got into my seat belt.

By the time I was buckled in, we went bouncing down over the rear car. Again, the force of the van's antigravity rods caused the car to screech and go out of control. This time, rather than going off the road, the car bounced end over end and rolled around umpteen times. The bag ladies in that car must have felt as if they'd been in a centrifuge at the high setting after that.

No one in the car moved when it finally landed on its top and played dead.

The car Jake was in had come to a quick stop as we passed over it. A spotlight from the car was turned toward us as we climbed out over the ocean and made a quick turn and headed back toward the remaining car.

"Any ideas?" Nikki asked as the bullets from the guns below us started dinging off the outside of the van and the windshield.

"Don't drop as low; we can't risk hurting Jake. But come in close. It looks like they left Jake in the car."

Nikki went over and the bag ladies standing on the road were flattened as we flashed over them. Nikki did a quick stop that felt as if it exceeded the limits on my seat belt if not my body and made a tight turn toward the car. This time we went over it slowly; a bag lady who had been struggling to her feet was instantly thrown flat onto the plastic roadway and knocked senseless. We circled it twice. No one moved below us.

Nikki flew out over the ocean and held the van at the same level as the car on the bridge. She turned the van's lights on so that they bathed the car on the road. A bag lady sat next to Jake; he appeared to be unconscious.

"Oh, no. I hope they haven't hurt him," Nikki said.

"Probably just stunned," I said, hoping it was the truth.

The bag lady jumped out of the car and went running down the road toward the city.

"Shall we chase her down?" Nikki said.

"No, let's get Jake. The rocket takes off in just minutes and we should get out of here as soon as possible anyway. She's not going to harm us now."

Nikki eased the van forward; the guardrail crumpled

under us as we went over it. Nikki settled the van down on the highway. I jumped out and ran to the car.

"Jake! Jake, are you all right?"

Only snoring answered my question. I pulled him from the van. I knew better than to try to lift his heavy frame; wearing a truss the rest of my life didn't appeal to me. "Nikki, can you give me a hand?"

She got out and ran alongside. Together we wrestled Jake into the van and got him buckled into the rear seat. We screwed his helmet onto his suit and I put a quick patch, from his suit's emergency kit, over the spot where the bag ladies' stun shell had hit him.

"Do we have to listen to his snoring?" Nikki asked over her suit's radio.

"We ought to keep track of him to be sure he's breathing OK," I lied. I figured there was nothing like hearing someone snore for a while to kill any romantic interest someone might have for him.

Behind us, the sky lit up around the rocket port.

"There goes our rocket," Nikki said and pulled off the road.

Just as we crossed over the water, fire covered the roadway, lighting the area as if it were daylight. As the fireball from the road climbed into the air, a fighter screamed over the road, causing the flames to roll as the air was torn aside by its passage.

Radar had picked up our battle with the bag ladies. Now someone was aiming to even up the score.

24

"Oh—Let's get out of here!" I yelled over the radio as the fighter wheeled about to make another pass at us.

Nikki didn't need any encouragement. I fell back into the seat as we flew forward at maximum speed.

"Get the radar on them," Nikki said.

"Good idea." I struggled to overcome our acceleration and get my hand to the switch to turn on the machine. Then I had to turn the antenna to pick up what was behind us.

"Let me know if they fire any missiles."

"They have those?"

"You better believe it," Nikki said. "I imagine he's holding off because he doesn't know what he's dealing with. But when he sees that we can keep up with the rocket, I'm sure he'll try to get us by—"

"Here come two," I said as I saw two small blips break off of the larger one behind us.

"Two! Can't outmaneuver two," Nikki said. "I've heard pilots talk about those. The new programs take alternate routes. One will always get you. How much time?"

"Coming fast. About . . . oh . . . three seconds away, at a guess."

I counted mentally as I watched the blip come racing at us: three, two—

The van shuddered as Nikki flipped a switch on the control computer then jammed the van's controls to cause it to go straight up (though our momentum kept us going forward as well). The metal skin of the van groaned; it was designed for low air resistance when it traveled forward, but not if it went straight up.

The two blips caught up with us and started to circle upward but as they went below us, hit our antigravity field. I saw what Nikki was trying to do; deflect them with our repelling power. The missiles followed us but at ever slowing speeds. Finally, they started to lose the race, fell back, then suddenly veered downward, tumbling out of control as we traveled upward.

The missiles fell toward the ocean and each exploded in the distance, far below us.

"All right," I said. "Good job, Nikki. Oh-oh—another blip."

"How long until impact?"

"About eight seconds this time: seven, six, wait, now six . . . It's dropping off. We're outrunning it."

We left the missile behind and it finally ran out of fuel and dropped into the great Florida swamp with a brilliant flash.

Nikki pushed the van through a series of twists and we were following the rocket toward Houston.

Later, we found ourselves dropping down toward Houston to the tune of Jake's snoring. We were afraid we weren't close enough to the rocket to stay within its radar blip and we fully expected a fighter to be waiting for us when we reached the Houston field.

But there weren't any.

Nikki dropped us down on a road near the rocket port and we drove around to the huge parking lot and made our way toward the entrance of the rocket port buildings. As we slowed down, we met the sixteen people we had freed. We parked the van nearby and everyone gathered around us as we stepped out. They cheered and clapped.

I smiled a moment.

"Thanks. You're free men and women tonight. We can give each of you some cash, uh, we can borrow a little from Jake, he's the third member of our group and—"

"He caught a stun shell and is sleeping it off in the van," Nikki said.

"Yeah. Anyway, you're free to go if you want. But we're in the process of starting up a factory, to make the antigravity rods. We have a lot of plans, a trip to the asteroids to get water, a couple of Moon bases, maybe even a starship down the way. We need people like you. If any of my old team wants a job, or any of you other folks who were on the government's blacklist, I can give you one. The pay isn't much; in fact it's nothing right now. But you'll be as safe or safer than you'll be on your own. And you can keep anything you steal and get away with.''

They all laughed politely for a moment.

"I have a husband," said one of the women who'd been trapped in the elevator shaft with me. "I couldn't leave—"

"You're free to return to him," I said. "Just get some cash from us and head home. If you *and* your husband would like to join up—"

"I'd like that," she said.

"Yeah, well, any of you who have a family might want to head home, collect everyone, and then join us later."

"What about kids?"

"Well, if we set up a real colony on the Moon, I suppose we'll want some kids to keep it going," I said, even though the thought of mouthy little children getting into things made me have second thoughts about what I was getting into.

"Where do we meet you after we collect our families?"

Where? Good question. "Well, I guess you folks can keep a secret as well as anyone. Don't suppose there are many traitors among those that Dobrynin was about to cancel."

A nervous laugh this time.

"OK. Our meeting place is a military surplus store near Galveston." I gave them the directions to it. "Be there as soon as you can. After a week or two, I can't guarantee that we'll be there anymore. I suspect that there'll be quite a few folks trying to get us after today so we won't be staying there for long."

With that, six of the group left after I insisted that they take some of the cash we fished out of Jake's pocket to help them get to where they were going. I figured I could afford to be generous with Jake's money.

All of my old team stayed with me. They waited while Nikki and I purchased an old junker from a nearby used car lot and then we returned with it and everyone piled into it and the van (which meant we couldn't fly without endangering them).

Jake was still snoring when we pulled into the parking lot of his surplus store. And he didn't look a bit better after his long beauty rest.

We draped Jake across the table and threw the best coming-home party I'd ever seen.

When things were winding down, Nikki took my hand and led me out of the dining room turned party center.

I knew leaving Jake's suit radio on would pay off.

25

Things flew along quickly. Within a week, we had all the rods cut up and incorporated into a fleet of junk vehicles that were to fly our huge party to the Moon. (After looking over some of the cars and vans we'd be taking, I figured we would be making Earth about three percent more beautiful by leaving.)

Other groups of people worked equally hard. Our space-suit repair crew had all the suits that could be made workable in Jake's surplus business patched up and ready to go; air tanks were filled to full capacity to support our band during our jump across the black airless space between Earth and our lunar base. Those with electrical skills repaired old radios or rewired vehicle radios to power small speakers sewn into suits so we could all communicate while in space.

All in all, we would be traveling on a wing and a prayer with chewing gum and paper clips to hold things together. We'd be taking quite a party of people and equipment since more and more people had been coming in to join us. Not only did the original sixteen we'd freed from the prison show up, but their families, pets, children, and colleagues as well. As might be expected with all the people involved, word leaked out and we soon had old spacers wandering in with their own worn suits and needed skills asking if it was true that we were mounting a space expedition. We converted the vehicles they came to us in; we aimed to take everyone who really wanted to go.

In the evenings after we'd finished work for the day, old

spacers told their tales while the newer members talked of harvesting the asteroids, colonizing the moons of Saturn and Jupiter, or even creating a starship with the rods. The possibilities seemed limitless as dreams were spun into the small hours of the day and we started work again after a few hours of sleep laced with dreams of space.

There was a rush to get things done. We all knew it would only be a matter of time until word about the group we were collecting to take to the Moon got out. And soon after that, basic rebels that we were, we had little doubt that some zealous bureaucrat might well order a fleet of fighters to do a number over Jake's store. So everyone was pushing toward getting everything wrapped up so we could escape. There we felt we held the edge since Earth had dismantled its space program.

Once in space, we would be pretty safe because only Jake, Nikki, and I actually knew at which base we'd settled and started our operations. This meant that with a little luck our expedition could drop out of sight of the World Government.

After what seemed like an eternity of the hard work, we were nearly ready to leave.

"How's it going, Jake?" I yelled as I made the rounds with a cup of caffinex to keep me awake. The sounds of grinders and hammers made carrying on a conversation a tedious job.

A shower of sparks marked another weld on the car Jake was working on, then he flipped up the protective mask he wore. "Real well. This is the last of the fleet and it's nearly ready. It's lucky that a lot of the folks coming to us are bringing in their own computers."

"Yeah." We wouldn't have been able to fly all the vehicles if that hadn't happened. We had run out of money the first day we'd started this latest project and would have had no money to buy computers. "Even so, I wish we could have backup computers in each of the cars," I said as a group of workers pushed an old, rusty truck by us.

"Would be nice. But I don't think it's too risky. According to Danny Hill, the sun isn't spitting out much radiation right now so the computers should be pretty reliable."

"He should know."

"Guess we'll just cross our fingers for the flight."

"That's how I fly anyway," I said. "Know where Nikki is?"

"She was around here a minute ago," Jake said. "I bet she went up to our 'command center,'" he smiled and winked at me, then dropped his welding mask over his face and went back to work on the car.

I walked off to our so-called command center; it consisted of three phones and an inventory computer all on Jake's kitchen table, a huge bulletin board, and the ever-being-used caffinex machine. It had become the heart of our planning sessions and Nikki, Jake, and I spent all our free time there trying to coordinate our group's efforts.

Nikki hung up the phone and brushed her dark hair from her eyes. "Well, that's the last of them. I've contacted every major reporter we could think of. Our takeoff tomorrow should have a lot of coverage."

"I just hope it doesn't have a fireworks display as well."

"What?"

"An attack of some kind."

"I don't think anyone would be that dumb with the news people there. I think the general public is so fed up with high utility bills that they'll riot if it looks like someone's throwing a monkey wrench into things. Anyway, we've told everyone that we'll be in Houston. We'll give a last minute call tomorrow morning to reroute the news crews here in time for the takeoff. It'd be hard for the government to get organized in time to do much damage."

"Provided they don't get wind of what's going on. I hope that Frank Walsh really knew how to rig up the phones with his computer to make it impossible to trace our calls."

"I'm sure he does. He's the communications whiz, you know."

I looked at Nikki's beautiful dark eyes a moment. "It just bothers me. More and more, it seems like things are out of our hands and in the hands of the experts we seem to be attracting."

"That's the price you pay for launching the project that got all this going."

"I just wish I'd had a choice. Everything snowballed. I certainly don't mind losing a lot of my responsibilities. . . . It's just that . . ."

"Security is gone when you start depending on so many other people."

"Right."

Nikki reached over the table and held my hand. "Phil Hunter, you are one big worry wart."

"Compliments will get you nowhere." I looked at my fingernail watch. "Oops. Late again. If anyone needs me, I'll be with my team up in the loft. We have something we're cooking up."

"Sounds mysterious," Nikki said.

"Unbelievably. It looks like we've made a mistake in our calculations, I think. But I can't figure out where. And if we haven't . . ."

"Something wrong with the rods?"

"No, nothing to worry about. Just a side effect that occurs when you get a bunch of the rods together. We think."

"OK, be mysterious."

"See you in a bit."

She rolled her eyes, shook her head, then blew me a kiss as I left.

The air conditioner was pushing out waves of cold air as I climbed the ladder into the loft of the old barn. My five team members were arguing heatedly about something. They all stopped when my head got even with the loft.

"No need to stop for me. I like a good argument." I got all the way up the ladder and stepped onto the old wooden floor.

Marion Wescott adjusted the antique glasses that she insisted on wearing, and flipped back a lock of blond hair. "We went over it all again," she said, pointing to the projection screen tacked to the barn wall, "but it still comes out wrong."

I looked at the screen. "We've all assumed that we made a mistake. Maybe we should look at it as if it's correct."

"But . . ."

I raised a hand and everyone was quiet for a moment.

"Let's just assume that it's correct for now. We'll be able to test out our theory or formula or whatever this mess is shortly. The bots we left working on the Moon—if they haven't screwed up—should enable us to have enough rods to see the effect."

"But it doesn't seem possible that such a small gravity field could warp space that much!" Marion said. Everyone nodded.

"I agree. Yet it doesn't seem like the rods should work at all. Remember when we started? The thing that held us back for weeks was that we didn't think they could work. When we finally settled down and tried making some rods, they worked. And here we are today."

"So what shall we do now?" Tom Barrel, a tall, thin black in his twenties asked.

"I want you guys to generate all the information we'll need to . . . uh . . ."

"Warp space," Steve finished.

"Yeah," I said, looking perplexed. "It still sounds impossible doesn't it?"

They all laughed. Sometimes, that's the job of a good team leader—make the individuals relax so that they don't cut each other's throats.

"Well, to heck with the impossibility. Give me the calculations I'll need to set up . . . oh . . . let's call them gates. Give me the calculations to set up space-warping gates to get to each of the planets in our solar system. And maybe even a few of the close stars."

I looked at each of the young faces in front of me. It was beginning to sink in, I thought. We might be working out a way other than sub–light speed travel to quickly hop to the stars!

"What are we going to call this formula and theory?" Tom asked.

"That's simple," Marion said. "Hunter's Principle."

There was a murmur of agreement among the team.

"Let's don't worry about naming it right now," I said. I liked the sound of it but wanted to at least appear to be humble. "Just get the information generated so we can test this out when we get to the Moon.'' I left them, knowing that they'd probably give me much more than I was asking for.

Hunter's Principle. Not bad. And if the calculations proved correct, rather than being an intellectual dead end, our little Moon base was apt to change the course of human history even more than I cared to imagine.

26

The news conference was a letdown. It was as good as we'd hoped for. Better. Jake's lot was packed with news cars and vans. But I was tired of being in such a constant state of flux and was ready to be inconspicuously ordinary.

There were hundreds of reporters, each holding a mini-cam and asking a barrage of either intelligent or idiotic questions but never anything in between. After Nikki put the van through its paces for them, I could almost see the electricity flowing through each brain as they realized the possibilities of the rods. Nothing like an old van, pocked with bullet holes and dented from crashes, to blow minds as it does acrobatics in the air overhead.

"Here's something else of interest," I said after the van landed. "Monny Prell, a design engineer we've picked up, has rigged this little generator from the rods. Now, we'll hook up a couple strings of lights and some power equipment . . ." A bunch of us quickly had a string of appliances and lights running off the generator. "That's about what a small apartment uses. The cost of the generator, if they were produced on a large scale, would be about one week's salary. As you can see, for a small price, every home in the world could afford to make its own power for household appliances."

The questions stopped after that for a minute while everyone mulled it over.

"I'm having Tom hand out some little sections of rods we've cut out of the last of the rods we've made. I figured that having a little bit of a rod in your hand, trying to float away, would give you something to remember us by."

There was a mad scramble by each member of the crowd to get one of the rod sections. Tom had trouble keeping his footing in the jostle but finally got the sections more or less distributed to the reporters.

I talked a bit more, then finished up my sales pitch. "The time of massive generators, pollution, and terrorist acts that leave us . . . in the dark . . . are soon to be things of the past," I said. "Now I'd like—"

The reporters had recovered. Not willing to let me finish where I wanted to, they started calling out questions.

"Will you ever make flying belts for individuals?" asked a dark-haired woman toward the back of the group.

"We thought about that," I said. "But it's too dangerous. If you get your legs in the way, it can cause severe injury when the rods try to push your feet away from your body. Also, if you miscalculate just a little, it would be easy to drop like a rock. Someday we might be able to make an array of pin-size rods and have them controlled by miniature servomotors and a computer. Until then, though, a flying belt would be a terribly dangerous way of traveling."

I fielded a few more trivial questions, then Jake stepped up to the car that was serving as my stage and pointed to his fingernail watch. Time to go.

"One final thing," I said. "If each of you will focus your cameras on this sheet of paper . . ." Everyone did. "This won't make much sense to most viewers. It's the formula for making the rods. The process isn't quite as simple as the formula, but anyone with a little metallurgical knowhow can pull it off. Anyone watching out there has my official authorization to use my formula to create as many rods as they wish. They can use them privately or sell them for a profit. This is our—the research team that helped me produce this as well as myself—this is our gift to the world."

It will also take the heat off us, I thought; the genie was now out of the bottle as the formula was beamed at the speed of light to all the global communications satellites and from there to homes and offices around the world.

Jake stepped up beside me, "Sorry, folks, but that's all the time we have."

Amid some clapping and shouted questions that I did my best to ignore, Jake and I pushed our way through the crowd as each of our little band got into their assigned vehicles and our caravan of thirty-six cars and vans lifted off together.

We nearly squashed one gung-ho reporter who decided to try to get a shot from below the vehicles and instead got flattened by the gravity wash in the process. He struggled back to his feet with a broken camera and a bloody nose. He made a good object lesson for the folks back home as to how dangerous the rods could be.

I knew things were going too well.

And sure enough, no sooner were we in the air than a fighter dropped down, screeching over us with a sonic boom that visibly rocked the cars and vans floating in the hot Texas air. There was no way of knowing if the plane was really out to get us or to impress the news people; one canister of napalm then and there would have done it. I figured he must be aiming to spare the reporters and take out our space caravan. At any rate, the plane just went overhead on the first pass.

"Get going," I said into my radio to the other vehicles. "Get into your orbit as soon as possible. We'll hold this guy off here if we can and catch up to you as soon as possible. If we don't make it, the sealed envelopes we gave you will show how to program your computers to get to our base on the Moon."

The vehicles flashed forward and upward in the hot Texas air as I watched. The fighter was just slowing down enough to make a low-altitude turn and was headed back. The hot air made its distant image wave and flicker as it headed back toward us.

As the fighter approached, a missile dropped off its wing and came flashing toward us.

"Can you outmaneuver that?" I asked Nikki.

My head suddenly was flung back into the seat as our van leaped into the path of the missile—Nikki was trying to get it locked onto us rather than another of our group— and then she went through a series of heart-stopping turns that took us up and finally over the missile so that it was repelled downward to expend its energy and explode harmlessly in the earth below.

"I'm tired of being the victim," I said as we hovered in place, waiting for the plane to turn and head for us again. "Nikki," I said. "Take us down a bit—keep enough altitude so you can maneuver if you have to—then hold us real still. I need a shooting platform." I'd half been expecting trouble and had made it a point to learn how to use the rail gun. And I was getting *real* sick of seeing lousy fighter planes in action. Now I pulled out the rifle (I'd stowed it next to me for such an event).

"OK, now turn the van so my side's toward the plane," I said as I kicked the van door open, loosened my seat belt, and slid around in the seat so my feet hung out over nothing. I pointed the gun out the open door and focused the scope on the oncoming plane.

The fighter was gaining altitude in the distance, probably to send a missile in over us so we couldn't deflect it downward. Below us, the crowd of reporters scattered all directions while a few brave souls stood their ground and took pictures of what was happening above them.

A rail gun sends out a small projectile of depleted uranium wrapped in a steel shell. It travels so fast that even a plane is standing still for all practical purposes; the fighter was a relatively easy target. All I needed to do was center the plane in the crosshairs of the scope. The speed of the shell gave it the kinetic energy of a much larger projectile. Provided the plane and shell connected, the fighter wouldn't bother us again.

Provided they connected.

It seems like it would be simple to hit a plane from a stationary spot. It would have been; the problem was that the van wasn't stationary: the wind caused the van to sway ever so slightly—and my hands were shaking as well.

Like all handheld rail guns, it had only three barrels. I had to strike the plane with one of three tries or we were out of luck. So I lined the fighter up in the crosshairs the best I could and fired. The rail gun recoiled as the shell accelerated down its magnetic track.

I scored one miss.

I aimed and fired again. Another miss.

One shot left.

As I watched, a small missile dropped from the plane and started toward us. I lowered my aim. There was no need to hit the plane if the missile got us. I aimed at the missile and squeezed the trigger.

The missile exploded below the plane; the shrapnel from its premature explosion riddled the fast-approaching plane. Apparently the fighter's on-board computer was damaged for the plane suddenly tumbled end over end, out of control without the microsecond adjustments needed to keep it stable.

Nikki forced the van into a short dive and we flew under the tumbling inferno as it was carried through the air by the momentum of its flight. The fiery wreckage arced overhead and fell well behind us to cover the dry earth with bits of molten plastic and burning fuel.

"The news people got a nice show," I said as we stopped and hovered about ten meters off the ground. "OK, let's catch up with our group before we have another showdown." I tossed the now useless rail gun out the door and closed it. A small boy below ran over and picked it up as we pulled away; a souvenir he'd probably hang on his bedroom wall, I thought.

27

When we reached the Moon, we discovered that the bots had made a pile of antigrav rods the size of which I couldn't believe, partly because of a little trick Nikki had pulled.

She'd been messing with the computers and a small experimental manufacturing assembly she'd brought back from Eratosthenes Base when we'd gone parts raiding. Basically, it was a meter-sized cube that was an automated factory for producing computer memory modules in the near vacuum of the Moon. Coupled with the power provided by the rod generators we'd set up, which produced almost limitless electricity, the little factory had been chugging out computer memories on the side. And Nikki had programmed the bot overseeing the factory to plug them into the computer overseeing the bots and the mining/rod-making operation. The computer quickly become a super computer.

The computer wasn't fast by modern computer standards; that's impossible to achieve with modular units. But it was smart. And Nikki had fed an Oracle program into it so that it continuously analyzed what the bots were doing and made alterations in their programs to speed things up. The bots were turning out rods faster than we had ever thought possible.

And bots.

The Oracle computer had taken information from the mass information storage computer on the base and started a side assembly line, which was making new bots to be added to the work force. That surprised even Nikki but made perfect sense to the computer no doubt. More bots would, after all, further accelerate the process of creating rods.

While the rest of our convoy was getting settled into their small rooms in the base, Nikki and I stood outside in the slow lunar sunset and watched the activity of the bots as they dragged rods out on sleds. The rods were piled in a huge archlike arrangement that Oracle had come up with.

"You know, there aren't many of the original bots working," I said after we watched the process for a while.

"There aren't any that I can see," Nikki said. "Hey, Jake, you listening in?"

"I shouldn't be, but I am. Sorry."

"No problem. You inside the mining area?"

"Yeah," he said. "I know what you're going to ask. The answer is that there is one of the original bots in here. What happened to the others? Worn out?"

"Maybe," Nikki said. "But I doubt it. It would always be easier to use the repair program rather than completely replace the bot. Especially since the minifactory I set up is making the same standard memory units that Oracle and all the bots use."

"Can you check Oracle for what happened, Nikki?" I asked.

"Sure, I'm curious, too. I'll be back in a minute."

I watched her bound away then turned my attention to a pair of bots that pulled a load of rods from the plant toward the stack. Then I realized something rather strange was going on. Rather than pile the rods along the outside, the bots had been walking down the aisle formed by two stacks of the rods.

I followed the bots, curious about where they were headed. They made their way down the aisle, then made a left turn, right into what should have been a wall. "What the . . ."

They were gone for about five minutes while I tried to figure out what they were up to.

"What's going on?" Nikki asked, bouncing up to where I was standing.

"I don't know. See those bots coming out with the empty cart?"

"Yeah."

"They just walked through a solid steel wall of those rods or—"

"Or what?"

"Or Hunter's Principle. The rods are warping space. Hey, Jake, shut down the bots in there for a minute. I don't want any more rods brought out here to throw off the force field we've created."

"Will do," Jake's voice crackled over the radio. "What's up?"

"I'm not sure. I think Oracle may have managed to create a space gate."

"A what?"

"Remember, we were talking about the possibility of warping space. Looks like maybe it *is* possible to do. I'm going to check it out."

"OK. I'll be out in a minute."

"Just be sure no one moves the rod arrangement around. That could change the setting. No telling where we'd end up."

"I'll come out and guard the rods so nothing's disturbed."

"Great. I'm going to take a look now," I said.

"Me, too," Nikki said.

I started to say no, then looked at her through her bubble helmet. With that look on her face, I thought, it would be crazy to try to talk her out of exploring with me.

We bounced toward the rods, casting long shadows on the crater floor. "Did you find out what happened to the bots?" I asked.

"Each one was lost."

"Lost? How would—"

"Every time they added rods to the outside while bots were between the piles of rods—here in this valley or aisle"—she said as we walked in the area between rods—"they would disappear. Finally, Oracle quit adding rods to the outside and started storing them inside. Even though there shouldn't have been room."

"Just so they could get the rods back and quit losing bots, there was no reason for the program to question how it worked."

"Exactly. And they quit losing bots after that."

"The rods added on the outside must have changed the coordinates."

"The coordinates of what?" Nikki asked.

"Of the gate," I said. "The bots that were lost must have gone . . . but that would mean that somewhere there are other gates."

"Which means?"

"Which means that someone—or something—is already building the gates. Sure you want to come? We might be meeting a bot-eating monster," I said as we neared the blurred area ahead of us.

"You can't scare me, Phil."

"Jake," I said. "We're entering the field now."

We both remained speechless as we stepped into the blurred area and headed down what should have been a wall of rods but looked like a long black tunnel. The darkness seemed to shimmer and made my eyes hurt whenever I glanced at it. "Jake, can you read us?"

Nothing. I stopped for a moment. "What do you think?" I said to Nikki.

"If we were smart, we'd probably go back."

"If we were smart is a little iffy, right now."

"Yeah. Let's go on and see what's making that rainbow ball of light ahead of us."

The sphere of light was beautiful. The calculations said the rods warped space. Period. They did more than that. They created one of the most beautiful displays of changing patterns of light ever seen by human eyes. The ball of light danced ahead of us as we neared it, then it proved to be a hole into which we stepped. Our bodies seemed to become part of the interplay of shapes and colors. Almost with regret, we stepped out of the gate and felt a heavy, Earth-weight gravity.

"Look at that!" I said as we both stumbled to regain our footing under the heavier pull of the gravity. We certainly were no longer on the Moon. Wooded areas were broken by long expanses of grass. The plants were growing wild and looked like the old pictures of Earth. Butterflies the size of footballs fluttered about while a strange whirring insect or small animal occasionally zipped by on an unknown task.

At first I thought we were back on Earth. But the small animals and greenish sky told me we weren't. And everything had two shadows; I sneaked a peek at the sun. "Binary sun?" I said. "Where do you suppose we are?"

"There're the rods, anyway," Nikki said and pointed to a huge stack of rods several meters away resting in a clump of trees. "And what do you suppose that is?"

I looked where she pointed. In the distance, a blue, lacy crystal mountain appeared to be floating in the air. Large budlike areas seemed to grow out of the narrow tubes connecting everything. The size was deceptive—it had to be huge, judging from the hazy look it had, which could only have been caused by our distance from it.

"That," I finally said, "is what a city looks like when the culture building it has antigrav rods."

"Do you suppose it's inhabited?" Nikki asked.

"If it is, they must be the most uncurious beings living in the universe. I can't imagine having this gate with bots coming through it all the time and not checking up on them."

"Abandoned?"

"Maybe. We'll have to see later on. For now, we'd better get back," I said.

"Yeah."

We turned toward our entrance. Unlike its counterpart on the Moon, this one was created by two monoliths of blue stone, apparently designed just to be a gate. A stargate, since we were somewhere far, far from Earth. An alien control panel—or perhaps just an elaborate work of art—stood in front of it, glowing with a changing pattern of small lights.

We walked toward the gate and stepped into the blurred area that marked the entrance and moved back into the shimmering darkness. We walked without talking.

We didn't step out on our Moon. It was an airless, barren world. But not the Moon.

"What's going on?" Nikki asked.

"I don't know. But I think I know how the bots got lost. Let's backtrack real quick."

We started at a walk and ended in a run. We stepped back out on the planet with the blue crystal city in the distance.

"We'd better sit tight for a while," I said. "They'll surely start sending bots through the stargate we created on the Moon. Then we can follow one of the bots back."

We waited.

Hours passed while we explored the area around us.

We slowly ran out of air in the suits' tanks.

"Do you think it's safe to breathe the atmosphere?" Nikki asked.

"There isn't much alternative. I did notice that some of the plants . . . Look there, if that isn't a dandelion. . . . So maybe."

We cracked our helmets open and tried a quick breath. We didn't die right away. We removed our helmets. Hours later, it appeared that the air was safe. I hoped we hadn't picked up some weird virus or fungus that would kill us later on. I decided to keep that worry to myself.

"They'll get to us before long," I said as I put my arm around Nikki and one and then the other sun sank below the horizon and foreign stars dotted the purplish sky. We put our gloves and helmets back on as the air turned cool.

When we awoke the next day, there still wasn't a bot to be seen.

At noon, alien planet time, a bot finally wandered through the gate with a load of rods as if it were business as usual. We followed it back through the alien gate after it had deposited the rods in the pile and started back—we hoped—for the Moon.

We stepped out to look down the rows of rods to the barren surface of the Moon.

"We're back!" Nikki said as we bounced out onto the lunar surface.

Cheering rang out over our earphones.

"Get back into the dome, you two," Jake's voice crackled through the din of the voices. "You've got some explaining to do."

Epilogue

Days later we learned that the alien gate had a schedule of "rounds" it cycled through. If you didn't step into it at the right moment, you ended up on one of six different places. Fortunately, when Jake had seen that we weren't coming back, he'd gotten Oracle to send bots through the Moon's stargate according to the timetable the computer had created by hit and miss. That enabled us to come back with the bot when the alien gate had finally cycled back to the Moon's coordinates.

As the months passed, we figured out a few of the controls on the alien stargate and began exploring the ancient ruins of the civilization that built the stargate and city, only to vanish. While some of us explored, others managed to set up other gates on the Moon and Earth and after our rod-driven ship had made the long trips to set up gates on Mars, Venus, and Mercury, started exploring those planets as well. With other bot-driven ships headed for the moons of Jupiter and Saturn it would only be a matter of time before there was more real estate than mankind ever dreamed was out there.

And Tom Barrel and Marion Wescott were soon putting the finishing touches on the plans for a starship driven by antigrav rods. Such a ship will allow us to carry a stargate to another system and then travel to and from it in a matter of minutes. Mankind would soon be traveling across our galaxy as easily as they walked to the next block.

Nikki and I spent more and more time on the planet Oracle found. The plants and the few small animals on the planet were very similar to those of Earth and many are identical. Biology is out of our fields and I have no way to explain the similarities. Has evolution paralleled itself on all worlds with life or do we all have a common ancestor or even a common Creator? I like to think the latter, but that is faith and not my scientific background showing through. Who knows?

Though the alien culture had many strange and wonderful inventions, they never seemed to have created anything like a digital computer. They worked with a device similar to a slide rule and that was it.

Though we're planning on leaving most of the new planet as a wilderness area, a number of the bots have been programmed to farm several areas of its large plains under the direction of a second Oracle computer. I'm hoping they can harvest a crop of wheat soon.

At any rate, Earth's problems with food, energy, and room are coming to an end. As we spread out and duplicate the automated system of creating rods that we'd pioneered on our first Moon base, we'll be changing the whole course of human history for the better—I hope.

Soon mankind can quit worrying about where the food for the day will be coming from and get on with the task of exploring the universe.

DUNCAN LONG is a specialist in military hardware, with more than ten nonfiction books in print, most recently *Modern Sniper Rifles*. He has written numerous magazine articles on the subject, and edits "Directions," a self-sufficiency/survivalist newsletter. ANTIGRAV UNLIMITED is his first novel.

Mr. Long was born in Smith Center, Kansas, in 1949, but now resides in the small town of Wamego, Kansas, with his wife and two children. He earned his B.A. at Sterling College and his M.A. in music composition at Kansas State University, and has worked as a rock musician, a teacher, and a proprietor of a mail-order business, before retiring to write full-time. His hobbies include target shooting, hiking, and watching movies.

AVON FLARE BESTSELLERS

by BRUCE AND CAROLE HART

SOONER OR LATER   42978-0/$2.95US/$3.75Can
Thirteen-year-old Jessie is a romantic and ready for her first love. She knows that if she's patient, the *real* thing is bound to happen. And it does, with Michael—handsome, charming and seventeen!

WAITING GAMES   79012-2/$2.95US/$3.75Can
Michael and Jessie's story continues as they learn what being in love really means. How much are they willing to share together—if their love is to last forever?

BREAKING UP IS HARD TO DO
89970-1/$2.95US/$3.95Can
Julie and Sean don't know each other, but they have one big thing in common—they both are falling in love for the first time…and they're about to learn there's a world of difference between first love and lasting love.

and a new romance

CROSS YOUR HEART   89971-X/$2.95US/$3.95Can
Ignoring her friends' warnings, Angelica falls for Gary —the gorgeous new senior with a mysterious past—until she is forced to face the truth.